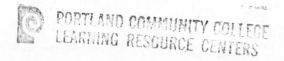

THE WALNUT TREES
OF ALTENBURG

André Malraux

THE WALNUT TREES
OF ALTENBURG

Translated from the French by
A. W. FIELDING

With a new Foreword by
CONOR CRUISE O'BRIEN

THE UNIVERSITY OF CHICAGO PRESS

Chicago and London

Originally published in French as *Les Noyers de l'Altenburg* in 1948 by Gallimard. Translation by A. W. Fielding first published in 1952 by John Lehmann, London.

The University of Chicago Press, Chicago 60637
The University of Chicago Press, Ltd., London

99 98 97 96 95 94 93 92   6 5 4 3 2 1

Library of Congress Cataloging-in-Publication Data

Malraux, André, 1901–1976.
    [Noyers de l'Altenburg. English]
    The walnut trees of Altenburg / André Malraux :
translated from the French by A. W. Fielding : with a
new foreword by Conor Cruise O'Brien.
      p.   cm. — (Phoenix fiction)
    Translation of: Les noyers de l'Altenburg.
    1. World War, 1914–1918—Fiction.
    2. Alsace (France)—History— Fiction.
    I. Title. II. Series.
    [PQ2625.A716N613   1992]
    843′.912—dc20   91–34670
                                CIP

ISBN 0-226-50289-9 (pbk.)

FOREWORD

A Meditation on Violent Death

IF OFFERED to English-speaking readers in the late twentieth century, without introductory explanation, *The Walnut Trees of Altenburg* would probably be puzzling, because it assumes a knowledge, which may well be lacking, of certain basic data of Franco-German history. In the first section of the book, datelined "Chartres, 21 June 1940," and in the last section, the narrator is a French prisoner of war. But the principal characters of the text in between—books I, II, and III of *Walnut Trees*—are the narrator's grandfather, father, and uncle, all of whom appear to be Germans. How come?

The answer to that one is simple. The narrator, his father, his uncle are all Alsatians. The province of Alsace, together with that of Lorraine, was sundered from France after the French defeat at the hands of Prussia and became part of the newly established German Empire (1871–1918). Books I and II are set in the early twentieth century (1908–12). Book III is set in 1915, early in the First World War. In both these periods, the people of Alsace, including the narrator's father and uncle, were subjects of the German emperor. In 1918, however, the German Empire collapsed after its defeat at the hands of the Allies. France recovered Alsace and Lorraine, and retained these provinces until her own defeat in 1940 (when Hitler reannexed them). The narrator was, accordingly, a French soldier and was captured along with many thousands of others in that year. (Alsace and Lorraine reverted to France four years later, after the defeat of Nazi Germany.)

The initial puzzle is therefore easily resolved. But under it there are other puzzles, which are more difficult.

Historically, Alsace, at the time of its annexation to the German Empire, had been part of France for nearly two hundred years. Most of its inhabitants still felt French and were, in varying degrees, restive under their new German government. There is hardly a sign of any of that in the early twentieth-century Alsace of *Walnut Trees*. It is mentioned that many Alsatians "placed their hopes in France," but no person actually belonging to that category makes an appearance in the book. It is stipulated that the narrator's father did not. *His* father was French, his mother German, and he tells us that "in the sphere of art and thought, at least, France and Germany were both necessary to him." The colloquium that is at the heart of the book is essentially a Franco-German colloquium. Friedrich Nietzsche, a supranational genius, is the tutelary intellectual deity of the book, and spokesman for the Spirit of Man. The most impressive contribution to the colloquium is that of the German nationalist Mollberg, who, we are told, "made German thought the designated interpreter of history; and Germany has, since Hegel, an uneasy and passionate gratitude for anything which makes of her the oracle of destiny." In books I and II, everything proceeds under the sign of Franco-German intellectual and artistic collaboration, with Germany as the senior party.

This idealized retrospect is puzzling enough in itself. The puzzle deepens, however, if we take into account the place and time of the book's composition. Malraux completed *The Walnut Trees of Altenburg* in June 1942. He was then living in the South of France under the quasi-autonomous, conservative, collaborationist, and devout Vichy regime of Marshal Pétain. In September of that year, Jean-Paul Sartre and Simone de Beauvoir called on Malraux to invite him to join the resistance. Simone de Beauvoir in *The Prime of Life* gives a short account of the meeting:

> Malraux received Sartre in a magnificent villa at Saint Jean Cap-Ferrat, where he was living with Josette Clotis. They lunched on Chicken Maryland, exquisitely prepared and served. Malraux heard Sartre out very courteously, but said that, for the time being at any rate, action of any sort would in his opinion be quite useless. He was relying on Russian tanks and American planes to win the war.

Between the wars, Malraux had been a hero of the Left, had worked with the Communists in China and Indochina, and had commanded the foreign aviators in the service of the Spanish Republic. His three "Asian" novels—*La Voie royale* (*The Royal Way*), *Les Conquérants* (*The Conquerors*), and *La Condition Humaine* (*Man's Fate*)— earned him the Prix Goncourt in 1933. *L'Espoir* (*Man's Hope*), reflecting his Spanish experience—or some part of that experience—followed in 1937 and consolidated his reputation as a leading left-wing activist and writer.

During this period—that of the Popular Front—Malraux, like many other French people who were not Communists, had cooperated closely with the Communists in a movement whose driving force came mostly from them. Trotsky even called him "a Stalinist agent." Malraux's own way of defending Communism was not in fact expressed in a manner calculated to earn Stalin's approval. At a dinner given in his honor by *The Nation* (Washington) in March 1937, Malraux declared that "just as the Inquisition did not affect the fundamental dignity of Christianity, so the Moscow trials have not diminished the fundamental dignity of Communism."[1] This was clearly the language of an ally who had become very restive indeed.

Jean Lacouture ascribes Malraux's disillusion with the Communist alliance to his experience in Spain. He compares Malraux's feelings to those of T. E. Lawrence—one of Malraux's heroes—when his Arab allies had, as he claimed, been betrayed by the realpolitik of the victorious Allies in the peace that followed the First World War.

---

1. Jean Lacouture, *André Malraux*, English translation (London, 1975), p. 230.

Lacouture asks whether "the problems of politico-military action, the results it yields, with all the bitterness, lies and deception it arouses, had haunted him since Spain, where he too had fought for something that had turned to ashes in his mouth?" (p. 299).

No doubt Spain had much to do with that, as it also had for George Orwell. But the Moscow trials—Stalin's "Inquisition"—had clearly played their part too. So must the signing of the Russo-German Pact in August 1939 also have done. Malraux refused to condemn the pact, in public. But he also refused—after Hitler's invasion of the Soviet Union—to join the Communist-led phase of the French Resistance, which was in progress throughout the year that preceded the completion of *The Walnut Trees of Altenburg*.

There is no trace in *Walnut Trees* of the left-wing commitment that had done so much to shape Malraux's activities and writings of the thirties. By his own standards of that decade, it is an "ivory tower" book. *Walnut Trees* was supposed to be the first volume of a larger work called *La Lutte avec l'ange* (*Struggle with the Angel*). Malraux claims in the opening sentence of his prefatory note that the sequel was destroyed by the Gestapo (presumably after the German occupation of the former Vichy state, in November 1942). This may be so—though Malraux may also, as Lacouture seems to suggest, have destroyed it himself. If the Gestapo did destroy it, it was hardly for ideological reasons (unless it was very different from *Walnut Trees*). If *Walnut Trees* had been submitted pseudonymously for publication during the Vichy period, it would have probably been cleared. The picture of Franco-German intellectual cooperation, and of the futility of war, would have been quite congenial to the censors, coming from an unknown author. Coming from the "dangerous Red," André Malraux, it would probably not have been accepted. In any case, it was not offered. *Walnut Trees* was first published in neutral Switzerland, and was not published in France until after the war, in 1948.

Malraux joined the Resistance at the end of March 1944, nearly two years after the completion of *Walnut Trees*. He joined after a Resistance group that included his younger brother, Roland Malraux, had been arrested on 21 March at Brive in the Corrège. Malraux attached himself to the British-backed networks of the Maquis, but he was also greatly esteemed by other Maquis groupings. The fact that he had never (at this point) broken *publicly* with the Communists undoubtedly helped him to consolidate his authority, as he did, over wide sections of the divided Maquis. Taking the clandestine name of "Colonel Berger," after the T. E. Lawrence-like Franco-German hero of *Walnut Trees,* Malraux played a brilliant part in the final phase of the Liberation.

That Resistance role, however, lay well in the future when *Walnut Trees* was written. The reader should be on guard against reading "Resistance" implications into a work that is, in reality, singularly free from anything of the kind. Nor was Malraux in this period affected by the exalted French nationalism that he later inhaled as an admirer and follower of General de Gaulle. Roger Stéphane, who called on Malraux at Cap d'Ail at the end of September, found that Malraux then "set little store by nationalism." And this is implicit throughout *Walnut Trees*. Vincent Berger, the book's hero, describes himself as "not much of a patriot." The book is the product of a period in Malraux's life during which he felt himself to be without power to shape events and withdrew temporarily into a partly ironic, partly obsessive, contemplation of the life of action, and in particular of violence. My own guess is that this contemplation may have been developed in the second part of *La Lutte avec l'ange,* and that Malraux destroyed that part because it did not square with his later Resistance role or with the political role that was open to him after the Liberation. *The Walnut Trees of Altenburg* had already been published, but the author could carry that one off, with great *panache,* through his Resistance role as "Colonel Berger."

The climate of (pre–World War I) Franco-German understanding may seem disturbing against the background of the period in which the book was written. The author was probably imagining, in historical retrospect, a happier future time, after the fall of Hitler, when it would again be possible for French and Germans to live together as friends. He was sensing the possibilities that were to come to fruition in the European Community.

2

SEVERAL readers have found *The Walnut Trees of Altenburg* disappointing. Jean Lacouture, Malraux's sympathetic yet somewhat skeptical biographer, contends that the book "has never emerged from the humble condition of a ruined temple which the builder uses to quarry stones." As a verdict on an incomplete work of fiction, this may be accepted. Yet there is more to *Walnut Trees* than that. As the title to this Foreword implies, I regard the book as essentially a meditation on violence. Malraux himself, like Yeat's Cuchulain, was thought of as "a man violent and famous." At the time he was writing this book, he had detached himself (temporarily) from the practice of violence, but was obsessed by the thought of it. The unity of *Walnut Trees* is the unity of that obsession.

The opening and closing sections of the book—prologue and epilogue, though not so announced—are about prisoners of war. The book is inserted, as it were, between brackets of defeat. These sections, in "Chartres Camp," are more autobiographical than anything else in the book. Malraux himself was taken prisoner near Sens in June 1940; Sens, like Chartres, is the site of one of France's great cathedrals. What seems to be implied is the transcendence of human misery through art, and, within that effort, the transcendence of violence, through thinking about it and writing about it. It is significant that *Walnut Trees* not only opens but also closes in a prison camp. Although Malraux had escaped from the camp at Sens, he escaped only into a more open type of camp: Vichy France, during the German occupation of northern and western France. The Nazis could close down Vichy any time they chose, by occupying it. They did occupy it in November 1942, five months after *Walnut Trees* was completed.

War is not the only form of violence that is the subject of meditation. There is also suicide. Malraux's own father had committed suicide (in 1930), and the suicide of the narrator's grandfather provides the theme of the opening pages of book I of *Walnut Trees*. Respect for suicide—by those who do it "firmly"—is enjoined. Within book I, as in *Walnut Trees* as a whole, there is a circular pattern. The first book closes, as it began, with the suicide of the narrator's grandfather.

The hero of book I—and, though not quite in the same sense, of the whole work—is the narrator's father, Vincent Berger. Vincent is a professor at the University of Constantinople and he is also a semi-independent agent of the German imperial government inside the Ottoman Empire after the fall in 1908 of the last sultan, Abdul Hamid II (nicknamed "Abdul the damned" in the West). Vincent is also described as "a bit of a shaman" (*un peu chaman*). "Shaman," as used here by Malraux, appears to mean a charismatic, dramatic personality: what in English we would call "a showman," though there is of course no etymological overlap. But Vincent, as well as being a shaman, is also something of a counter-shaman, for he gives his son the advice, "Man's most effective weapon is to have reduced to a minimum the element of showmanship in his character" (*réduire sa part de comédie*).

Both Vincent Berger and his creator, André Malraux, had problems with that advice. Vincent becomes friends with Enver Pasha, one of the leaders of the Young Turks who were to take over in Constantinople after the fall of the sultan. The German military somewhat distrust Enver: "his romantic violence was suspect in their eyes." But this is precisely the quality that appeals to Vincent Berger, who becomes Enver's confidential agent. In 1910, when the Italians try to take over Libya from the enfeebled Ottoman Empire, Enver, on Vincent's advice and with his assistance as well as with German backing, successfully mobilizes the desert tribes of the interior against the Italians, who put prices on the heads of both Enver and Vincent. In Vincent's case, the price is in "the name the Arabs gave him: *Le Tranchet.*" [2]

Vincent Berger is clearly modeled on Lawrence of Arabia, a shaman if ever there was one. Lawrence was a brave, resourceful, and histrionic guerrilla leader whose exploits were greatly magnified by the combined needs of Hollywood and British Intelligence in the immediate aftermath of World War I. The war in the Middle East was really won by the main body of the Allied Forces under General Allenby, Lawrence's Hashemite Bedouin irregulars having played a strictly ancillary role. But Allenby, advised by Intelligence, wanted to take over Syria, which the British government had earlier promised to their French allies under the secret Sykes-Picot Agreement of 1916. The

2. *Tranchet* is the French word for two tools that have different names in English: "Anvil cutter" and "paring knife." Enver Pasha (1881–1922) was a historic figure whose role in Libya was more or less as described. Vincent Berger, at Enver's side, is Malraux's creation.

British could not, because of that agreement, simply take Syria and then refuse to hand it over to the French. Instead, they put on a colossal charade, on the basis of which they would claim that Syria had not been conquered by British imperial forces—which was in fact the case—but had been liberated by the Arabs themselves. To lend some verisimilitude to this audacious fiction, Allenby ordered his victorious forces to hold back from Damascus (or, in the case of the Australians, to withdraw from it after they had actually taken it) and to allow Lawrence and his Bedouins in. "The Arabs had taken Damascus," so its future was no business of the French.

Malraux, born in 1901, was eighteen when the Lawrence legend was breaking on the world. As a Frenchman he must have been aware of the fictional element in it, but that did nothing to decrease its attraction; on the contrary. Lawrence appealed to him, both as an authentic hero and as a successful charlatan. Many years afterward, Malraux related his early dreams of the legend of Lawrence, "the dazzling legend of a Queen of Sheba army with its Arab partisans deployed beneath flying banners among the jerboas of the desert, and imaginary battles in the defiles of rose-red Petra."

At one time, Malraux had taken such dreams for reality. On 7 March 1934, after a flight over Yemen, Malraux had announced: "Have discovered legendary capital Queen of Sheba stop twenty towers or temples still standing stop at the northern boundary of the Rub El Khali stop have taken photographs for L'Intransigeant stop greetings Corniglion—Malraux."

The alleged discovery was later developed in seven articles with photographs in a popular Paris newspaper. Lacouture, writing in 1987, comments: "Thirty-three years later, neither the word 'discovery,' nor the idea behind it can stand up to examination. Not a single specialist of the southern Arabian world takes either the touched-up photographs or the fantastic reportage seriously."

Even Malraux's admirers acknowledged that he had his *côté farfelu* (dotty, bizarre, eccentric side). By 1942, when he was writing *Walnut Trees,* the *côté farfelu* was less in evidence as compared with the extravagances of the early 1930s. Malraux acknowledged to himself the need to reduce it still further, as appears from the advice to reduce "the element of showmanship." But he is in no hurry about that: the whole of book I is written under the sign of Lawrence of Arabia. Lawrence's public career had ended in theatrical disillusion over the supposed betrayal of King Feisal, through the failure of the Allies to provide a throne for him in the city his Bedouins were supposed to have conquered. Vincent Berger's last mission also ends in noble disillusion.

This was a mission to Central Asia in the hope of fulfilling a dream of Enver Pasha's. The dream was that of constituting a pan-Turanian empire, the Turanians being the peoples of Central Asia believed to be related to the Turks. Vincent Berger plunges on into Central Asia "from steppe to steppe," a Lawrence on a greater scale, to find his Lawrentian disillusionment: "Turania did not exist." Vincent returns to Europe. At Marseille an epiphany

xvi

awaits him in the form of an interview with a gangster about what it is like to kill someone: "The individual killed is of no importance. But afterward something unexpected happens; everything has changed, the most ordinary things, streets for instance, dogs . . ." Vincent then goes home to Reichbach in Alsace, where, five days later, his father commits suicide.

3

BOOK I is under the sign of T. E. Lawrence. Book II is under the weightier, more baleful sign of Friedrich Nietzsche. The narrator's Uncle Walter, a disciple of Nietzsche, makes his appearance. He and Vincent discuss the suicide of their father. Walter claims that he personally has shaken off the fear of death, but Vincent is sure that Walter is lying: "he was aware of anguish coming just to the surface." Walter speculates on how it could be that their father could commit suicide but leave a note behind asking to have a religious funeral. Was it fear? asks Walter. Vincent suggests humility. "Man is what he hides," Walter thinks. To which Vincent responds, "Man is what he does."

Vincent believes that whatever "cause" there may have been for the suicide is less important than "the resolution by which he had *chosen* death, a death which was like his life." (Malraux's own father, Fernand Malraux, who committed suicide in 1930, had been a tank commander in the First World War.)

Walter goes on to tell of his hero, Nietzsche. One

might think—because of the tension established between the two brothers—that Vincent would resist the Nietzsche cult, but no: "My father loved Nietzsche more than any other writer. Not for his preaching, but for the incomparable generosity of intelligence which he found in him. He listened, uneasy, fascinated."

Walter tells how, after Nietzsche had gone mad (in 1889, the year Hitler was born, although Malraux does not note the coincidence), he and another friend were taking the invalid for a ride on a train. As the train goes through the St. Gotthard tunnel, mad Nietzsche starts to sing. His song is "sublime," a triumph for the human spirit, effacing the stars in the sky. Vincent is moved by Walter's eloquence, and his own thoughts take the same shape.

The cult of Nietzsche had been almost universal among European intellectuals in the period about which Malraux is writing, the early twentieth century. W. B. Yeats wrote of Nietzsche, around then, as the "strong enchanter" and spoke of "the curious, astringent joy" he derived from reading him (a tribute that seems more relevant to Nietzsche than Vincent's vague "generosity of intelligence"). Almost all European intellectuals were under Nietzsche's spell when Malraux was growing up, and that the young Malraux should have fallen under it is not surprising. What may surprise is that he shows no disposition to question it in the circumstances of 1942. As a force in history, Nietzsche's "preaching" cannot be set aside from the rest of his work, as Vincent Berger tries to do. Nietzsche's originality and the source of much of his appeal lay in the fact that he was a revolutionary thinker in the sphere of ethics. The Enlightenment had attacked the supernatural aspects of Christianity but respected its ethical content: compassion, tolerance. Nietzsche's innovation was to attack, not merely the Christian religion, but specifically the Christian ethic as a confidence trick practiced by the Jews against the martial Aryans in order to weaken them. The Christian emphasis on mercy reversed the true Aryan values: "pride, severity, strength, hatred, revenge." These values would have to be restored.

Nietzsche was not just the property of the intellectuals, such as those who take part in the colloquium of book II. His revolutionary ethical message was widely diffused, with the encouragement of the German military authorities under the Empire and, later, with the encouragement of the Nazis, who believed themselves to be restoring the true Aryan values as prescribed by Nietzsche. The Holocaust, the logical culmination of that program, was already in operation (though hardly yet known about in southern France) when *The Walnut Trees of Altenburg* was being written.[3] It is argued, of course, that the Nazis were acting on a perverse interpretation of Nietzsche's teaching. Perhaps so, but the thought that they were so acting with horrible energy while the uninhibited and vague intel-

3. The view that Nietzsche's teachings played a major part in the ethical conditioning for the Holocaust is developed in chapter 1, section viii, of my book *The Siege: The Saga of Israel and Zionism* (New York, 1986).

lectual celebration of Nietzsche was being penned for book II gives a curiously eerie, airless, and disconnected feel to these particular passages.

The central message of book II is contained in the following reflection of Walter's, after he has completed his Nietzsche anecdote: "The greatest mystery is not that we should have been thrown by chance between the profusion of matter and that of the stars; it is that in this prison we may draw from ourselves images sufficiently powerful to deny our nothingness."

This reflection furnishes the leitmotiv of the colloquium which fills most of the remainder of book II. It was to be the theme that engrossed Malraux in his postwar studies of the history of art. And it prepares the way for the two closing sections of *The Walnut Trees of Altenburg*.

4

BOOK I is under the sign of T. E. Lawrence, book II under that of Nietzsche. Book III is under the sign of Tolstoy. Vincent Berger, hero of romanticized war in book I, confronts the horror of real war in book III. The description of the gas attack on the Russian front in 1915 will never be forgotten by anyone who has read it. This is not exactly a meditation on wounds and blood. The specific horror here is that, as Vincent Berger notes, "There were no wounds. No blood." Violent death assumes a pure, an abstract form. Malraux, in this unique passage, writes with the precision, the certitude, and the authority of an obsessed person who knows that he has found the essence of what he has been looking for. Vincent, returning from the gassed area, with its vegetation "like cooked salad," to the world of the living, has this epiphany: "Suddenly the memory of the Altenburg crossed my father's obsession: he was looking at great clumps of walnut trees."

The reader's horror on reading the description of the gas attack is deepened by knowledge of something of which Malraux himself was almost certainly unconscious at the time he wrote that description. On 20 January 1942, the conference at Wannsee, Berlin, coordinated the execution of the Final Solution. While Malraux was writing that description in southern France, the gassing of millions of human beings, of both sexes and all ages, had already begun in German-occupied eastern Europe.

The final section of the book, a return to the camp at Chartres, is under the sign of Pascal, whom the narrator quotes near the end:

"Once more Pascal comes to mind: Imagine a great number of men in chains, and all condemned to death; some of them have their throats cut in the sight of the others, those who remain see their own condition in the fate of their likes. This is the image of the human condition." The narrator, in the closing pages of the book, turns away from Pascal and finds matter for consolation, celebration, and even exaltation in the contemplation of the human condition. It is an eloquent passage, but Pascal is somehow still there, and so is book III. Malraux's affirmations of Life ring a bit hollow. What he writes well about is Death.

For my part, the image that will always stay with me out of *The Walnut Trees of Altenburg* is that of the little riderless horse galloping into the advancing sheet of poisoned fog, at the beginning of the gas attack.

NOTE

The continuation of Jacob Wrestling,[1] *the name under which I originally conceived my novel, was destroyed by the Gestapo. A novel can hardly ever be rewritten. When this one appears in its final form, the form of its first part,* The Walnut Trees of Altenburg,[2] *will no doubt be radically changed. This edition, then, will appeal only to the curiosity of bibliophiles and to those who are interested in "what might have been".*

One more word. The urge to be happy, which overwhelms Vincent Berger when he realises he is gassed, was taken by some critics, when this book appeared in Switzerland, to be the answer to the questions put in the first part of it. The urge to be happy is here simply a psychological reaction.

The text follows that of the original edition, after the deletions of the Swiss censorship.

A.M.

[1] La Lutte avec l'Ange.
[2] Les Noyers de l'Altenbourg.

CONTENTS

Chartres Camp

Chartres, 21 June 1940

I CANNOT make out the shape of the cathedral; the panes that have replaced the stained glass in the nave rip it open with sunshine. Down below, in the chapels, the narrow windows like pillars of light shake from top to bottom under the tidal roar of the German tanks streaming past. Like the wounded prisoners in front of me, like those behind, I am intrigued by the floor being covered with what we never expected to see again: straw. In the crowded nave, shivering, as it seems, in the flickering light, there are soldiers opening blood-caked tins of food; and others brandishing bottles, next to an abandoned Red Cross counter covered with drugs and dressings. We slump on to the sheaves of straw, whose stalks also quiver from the tanks rattling away as far as the borders of Beauce.

High up above me I can see where the great Gothic mouldings meet. My legs, which have become a yielding, paralysed sheath from the wound in my hip, melt away as they did in the field of clover when we were lying in wait for the enemy armour. By my side an Algerian

11

rifleman blankly watches the flies that come to settle on his face, and grins at his straw. Behind my head voices growing fainter and fainter talk of treachery.

A tickling stab in my foot wakes me up; a medical orderly prisoner is changing my dressing. He has taken over the bandages, the cotton-wool and peroxide left behind by the Red Cross and from the central doorway (we collapsed close by) he is looking after the wounded, whether they are asleep or not. Sparkling afternoon sunshine bursts through the lofty windows: I am inside the framework of Chartres under construction. Germans walk by, and those who are not asleep follow them with their eyes: has what they are saying something to do with the prisoners? In this world from which all news has vanished, every German is an oracle. I listen to the nearest one:

"At Bamberg, to the left of the cathedral, I know a little shirt-maker, *mein Kerl*, a shop-keeper who . . ." Bamberg, the Chartres of Germany. The misery of recognising what we share as brothers, between the cries of our wounded for the medical orderly and the noise of those jackboots disappearing!

Stirred by their passing, the rumours spread.

"Seems the armistice is signed. They're demobilising, but all the arms factories will have to work against the English . . ."

"Pétain has been killed by Weygand, right in the middle of a Cabinet meeting . . ."

"Here, I say, 'they' have taken over seventeen counties! Those sods of Bretons are in luck again!"

The Bretons, generally regarded up to now as "clods", are the object of universal envy: how could Hitler annex Brittany?

"The autonomists, they must've been in on the deal!"

"What about us, don't you think we could wangle it and be made Burgundy autonomists?"

"The Town Major went by just now. I understand German a bit; he said there were a million and a half prisoners."

Laughter all round: why not ten million?

The laughter suddenly dies: by the doorway two of the wounded have got to their feet, and straightaway ten, fifty; the milling swarm, each staggerer first protecting his wound, makes a rush for the Red Cross counter. Leaning on their elbows, the stretcher-cases follow this feeble stampede with the pathetic gaze of paralytics; presently a hundred cracked voices, echoing from the vaulted roof, yell:

"We've got permission to write, you chaps!"

I get up, hanging on to my stick with both hands, as though I were making use of a tree. Exhaustion has seeped back, crushing but human, and no longer that delirious weakness which kept us marching on with gaping fish-faces or made us clench our teeth. Another tank-corps casualty and I move up, leaning on each other like a pair of entangled crabs; on to the counter, which is now guarded by three N.C.O. prisoners, dozens of letters have already been chucked in a heap. Above it, a notice-board specifying what is allowed to be written: *I am a prisoner—I am wounded— I am well—I am being well treated—*

Best regards—Cross out what does not apply—No address to be given—Envelopes to be left unsealed.

By the time we reach the counter and turn round into the indiscriminate uproar of the wounded in which absurd questions mingle with angry demands for envelopes—"a bit of paper, there's bound to be some about" —the news has spread as far as the choir. And from one end of the cathedral to the other, delirious once more, distraught, fearful of not arriving in time, bent over sticks, clinging on to shoulders, leaving trails of blood behind them, the wounded surge towards two voices shouting alternately near the central doorway, like prophets chanting: "I am being well treated! Best regards!", while another thunders: "Cross out what does not apply! No address! Unsealed! Stop milling around like that, all over again! Good God almighty, there's room for everyone!" The horde of casualties slithers towards us, surges round this highest of high places on earth, until the voices soon get hoarse and resemble only the appeals of the beggars we used to see by the porch.

They are lost in the fresh rumours encountered at every step we take to get away.

"They say they've first got to go to Berlin, the letters, to be censored."

"Reynaud's in America and Flandin has taken over command of the war with Pétain."

"Nonsense! Pétain and Weygand have been arrested by Mandel!"

When we eventually succeed in leaving our envelopes on the pile, which is now enormous, the N.C.O.s can

only shout: "But you've been told that only those following the specimen copy will be sent!" And, clear of the
scuffle, I can see two prisoners who, after scattering their
straw to get down to the St. Louis flagstones, are now
lying flat on the floor writing endless letters.

I am pushed aside: a squad of Germans marches in: the
interpreters yell, their voices echoing from the historic
vaults:

"Pick up your things! In column of fours!"

They no longer dare to say "your packs".

From the cathedral, from the town, from the churches
as far as the Loire, from wherever they were defeated,
over five thousand men have been assembled in a vast
public works yard, and there are fresh arrivals every hour.

"Sleep in the field!" the interpreters shout.

The next morning, there is no longer a yard: it is the
compound. The two vegetable plots which bordered the
"field" have disappeared: not a sorrel, onion, cabbage,
seed-potato left: only grass or earth. Pink-coloured flames
are blazing in the dawn sky. One smart fellow has found
some rabbit-hutch doors of trellis-work, converted at
once into a grill. Not every prisoner has been captured,
like us, without his pack: mess-tins are appearing. And
vast circles of faces leaden from hunger and sleeplessness,
with a week's growth of beard, watch in silent envy the
few makeshift cooks toasting their last biscuit or boiling
up a witches' brew. In two days' time no doubt the bright
lads will be floored by their own fires.

Since there are bricks, the building of dug-outs starts.

There is a sense of ownership about already: Senegalese in helmets, Arabs in fezzes, Frenchmen in helmet-linings like Chinese skull-caps, go in search over the sprawling bodies, into the furthest corner, into the furthest heap, for the last empty tin or the last broken clock "which may come in handy". Some fellows who have only found a few bricks have marked out their personal territory and sit dreaming, their knees clutched between their hands, in the middle of their imaginary kingdom.

One of the most common gestures in the camp is that of a prisoner rummaging at the bottom of his pocket and lifting his hand to his mouth; he has found a bread-crumb. For the last five days most of the prisoners have had nothing to eat but tiny scraps.

On leaving our shelter, my tank-corps friend and I find over a thousand prisoners lined up three yards behind the barbed wire. It is ten o'clock. On the main road, cars and large country carts are now slowly making their way towards Paris: the first returning wave of evacuees. And overloaded, exhausted bicyclists push past the German military cars at full speed. Not a single pedestrian: no one is alive yet—everyone is on the move.

The people in the carts and the cars either try not to look at the prisoners (how many have they seen already?) or else wave them a furtive, almost sheepish, good-morning. Lying on the ground, the prisoners listlessly return the greeting. A German sentry marches past at rare intervals: this side of the camp is over three hundred yards long. Occasionally a bicyclist throws a cigarette in: a scuffle starts at once. In the sunshine and the high wind the sentry marches back, more German lorries stop at the petrol point, and the prisoners lie down again.

All of a sudden, from one end of the camp to the other, with the swift, gliding movement of a cat towards lights, they all press forward against the wire barbs: those at the end have seen a woman on the road—on foot—carrying a bag.

Some of the sentries chase the passers-by away, for no one is allowed to stop in front of the barbed wire; others pretend not to notice. The bread-hunters know them all by now: this one will turn a blind eye. The woman approaches; overtaken from time to time by a bleak cart or by an armoured car, she comes very slowly down the middle of the road, waiting for the sentry to march past. He does so. Although the bread-hunters know that this particular sentry will not turn round, the woman does not, and she moves towards them, keeping a watchful eye on the German. They wait, restlessly stamping and shuffling round like any other animal starving in a cage. Her bag is open, her right hand plunges into it. "Go ahead!" "Go on, go on!" the prisoners shout in a dreadful tone of voice— as though they were trying to shout in a whisper. She watches them, keeps drawing nearer: the tank-corps man and I, fifteen yards behind the enclosure, can only see their backs, but I know that signs of the impending scuffle must be showing on their faces.

She walks past.

Past at least four or five clusters of men. She does not even dare to take the bread out of her bag. A little further on, there are the same signs of hunger on their faces.

17

At last—from fatigue, anxiety, fear of the sentry's return—with an effort she comes up to the wire, takes from her bag a loaf of bread which glistens in the sun.

"Share it!" she brusquely entreats them.

So many hands grasp for it, and no doubt with such a look, that she draws back, and the loaf falls outside the wire. In the roar of the prisoners not a word can be heard. She picks up the bread, throws it in at last, and slips away without looking at the men who, smeared with blood from the wire barbs, get to their feet and manage to slip away, a scrap of bread in their hands.

She will be back. It is always the same ones that come. Till eleven o'clock—which was once dinner-time—the whole camp is ablaze with useless, sacrificial fires.

We go to sleep for a few hours in our dens (at night the cold drives sleep away), then come back. The barbed wire intrigues us, too; beyond it is the land of the living. The road is deserted. The prisoners in front of it are as numerous as ever. Yet no one will come for several hours: it is twelve o'clock, dinner-time for those who are free. There are scarcely any more military vehicles, and even the ebb-tide of evacuees is about to stop. In these plundered towns, how do they all manage to find enough to eat? The prisoners are not even on the look-out any longer, but stand dreaming.

Long minutes, on the empty road in the summer sunshine; the wind is blowing bits of paper, leaves.

And all of a sudden some prisoners surge back, not from the edge of the camp but from the middle of the barbed wire fence, as though they were making off under the weight of some invisible burden. Yet no one has arrived—of that there is no question: we scan the road from one end of the camp to the other, and as far as the cathedral which dominates it. All the faithful friends of the barbed wire, all the stray prisoners, are massing together.

The formation of these groups, moving like whirling leaves, is fascinating: what invisible body is distributing invisible manna in this noonday sun? We rush up, also. The last to arrive hoist themselves on to others' shoulders, others jump up, catch something as it flies past: leaflets being blown from the main street by the wind which comes from the town and scattered along the sides of the road.

"Good God!" yells the tank-corps man. "This means peace!"

How many times since our capture have I heard: "Hitler has declared he will enter Paris before June 15th and peace will be signed before the end of the month"? From the furthermost dug-outs right up to us, they all hurl themselves on the bits of paper.

I catch one in mid-air: the wind is blowing hundreds of them along. It is an unsealed envelope, inside it a sheet of paper:

"*Mrs. Hardouin, Saint-Cirq—Lapopie, Lot. I am a prisoner—slightly wounded—well treated—I shall write as soon as we are allowed to—much love—Sylvain.*"

It is not peace that the strong wind is blowing over to us, it is our letters from the cathedral.

One o'clock. The time when prisoners write letters in their huts. Once they used to write them after dinner.

One of the letters brought by the wind was a long one: there was a fond hope that these were returned letters, letters which the Germans had refused because their instructions had not been followed. The prisoners have gathered a large quantity of them: almost all, alas, are word for word copies of the German specimen. The silence of summer descends on the camp.

Their people will not know whether they are alive or dead; they will know nothing of their people. As though this barbed wire, this Roman-camp stockade which is beginning to be built, did not separate them sufficiently from the world outside! Now these huts, these fires, these wandering Senegalese, these whiskered cap-wearers, these prisoners' cabins begin to assume some eternal quality in the noonday sun and the wind.

The tank-corps man has started to write again. I watch him pondering, the tip of his tongue showing, purple with indelible pencil:

"Are you keeping a diary?"

He looks up in a daze:

"A diary?"

Presently he understands:

"No . . . I . . . that sort of thing . . ."

And, as if he were stating the obvious:

"I'm writing to my wife."

In this Babylonian hovel, made of pillar-stumps, drain-pipes and branches, there are now three of them writing on their knees, crouched like Peruvian mummies.

A pioneer, no youngster, is sitting in the same position, but with his arms crossed, staring fixedly at the pillars. He is conscious that I am watching him, and slightly turns his head:

"I'm waiting for it to wear off, myself."

"What?"

"Everything. I'm waiting for it to wear off."

This man has one of those Gothic faces that are more and more numerous now that beards are being grown. The age-old memory of the scourge. The scourge had to come, and here it is. I remember the silent conscripts of September marching through the white dust of the roads and the dahlias of late summer, who seemed to be marching against flood, against fire; but peeping out from underneath that age-old familiarity with misfortune is man's equally age-old ingenuity, his secret faith in endurance, however, cluttered with disasters, the same faith perhaps as the cave-man used to have in the face of famine. "I'm waiting for it to wear off . . ." In this den of ours, drowsy in the noonday sun of eternity, the whispering voice of prehistoric man.

Is it the same animal endurance that keeps the others writing today? Pencils, paper, purple tongues are in evidence in every cabin into which I glance as though looking for a friend, and even outside, where a few isolated figures are pinning the paper to their knees with their left hand so that the wind may not blow it away with the torn-up letters.

How many days have I watched them like this in the barrack-room, filling page after page? Are they saying once again that the binder must be seen to, that the time between reaping and threshing must be spent mending the drain-pipes—endless repetitions which are their instinctive way of expressing their feelings? Their wives know all this just as well as they do. At this moment the men are as unconcerned about the drain-pipes and the binder as they will ever be on earth; but it is not only through words of love that devotion tries to express itself. In these letters which will arrive, today or one day, from the camps where two million French prisoners are waiting for the effect of their destiny to wear off, how many wives will recognise, in this talk about not forgetting sowing-time, the proud, concealed, glowering passion of those fingers clutching the paper as if it were about to be torn from their grasp, while the letters that are already dead go whirling along the main road?

In my youth I dreamt I was walking over a leaden countryside covered, like this camp, with pipes and broken tiles, and where there wandered, between fences of infinite perspective, a crowd of frosty, disembodied overcoats; an unknown friend, who sensed my anguish even though I uttered not a word, was whispering by my side as he vaguely pointed out these infernal shadows: "It's nothing, sir; it's the unconscious."

Every morning I watch thousands of shadows in the restless light of dawn, and I think: "It's mankind."

I thought I knew more than I had learnt because I had found in one faith the two conflicting elements, religious and political; I now know that an intellectual is not only a man to whom books are necessary, he is

22

any man whose reasoning, however elementary it may be, affects and directs his life. These men I am with, these very men have been living from day to day for thousands and thousands of years.

In the earliest days of the war, as soon as his uniform had blotted out a man's profession, I began to see these Gothic faces. And what now emerges from the wild crowd that can no longer shave is not the penal settlement, but the Middle Ages. That applies even to those from the Mediterranean whose faces I expected to be those of Greek fishermen, Roman builders: perhaps because the Middle Ages undertook to represent men, and we are not in the sort of place that yields gods. But the Middle Ages are only a mask concealing their past, a past so long that it prompts dreams of eternity. Their love is a secret, even to themselves; their friendship, the human warmth of someone at whose side one can lie down and rest without a word—an exchange of silences. Their joy, all blows and outbursts, has not changed since Breughel, since the fairy-tales; that slapping and that laughter, how the sound of them issues from depths more fathomless, more intriguing than all the knowledge we have of the human race, as intriguing as its endurance! A friendly priest here has told me: "All men at heart, whether they are believers or not, die in a muddled mixture of fear and hope."

Oh to fall into that heavy, mysterious half-sleep over which the present day and christianity itself rotate like the dust over our sprawling bodies, like our dreams! As a writer, by what have I been obsessed for the last ten years, if not by mankind? Here I am face to face with our basic essence. And I think once more of one of my father's sayings, which the constant presence of death has imposed on my memory, and on which captivity relentlessly makes my thoughts run:

"It is not by any amount of scratching at the individual that one finally comes down to mankind."

How close I feel to my father, now that certain moments in his life seen to have foreshadowed my own. I was wounded on the 14th, taken prisoner on the 18th; his fate in the other war—and on the other side—was decided on June 14th, 1915. Twenty-five years ago, almost to the day. He was not much older than myself when he began to feel the impact of that human mystery which now obsesses me, and which makes me begin, perhaps, to understand him. His memoirs, which are still awaited by some people but which will never come out—they have never been edited—were simply a mass of notes on what he called "his encounters with mankind".

Those encounters the tireless wind blows back to me, as it blows back at random my comrades' letters. So let me examine them, let me compare them with my own, while the pink earth-worms summoned by the evening dew creep out once more from the ground stamped hard by the feet of five thousand men—while life goes on until my enquiries mingle with his in the last fellowship of death.

In this place, writing is the only way to keep alive.

The Walnut Trees of Altenburg

I

I

MY father had been back from Constantinople for less than a week. The bell rang very early; in the semi-darkness of his bedroom, the curtains not yet drawn, he heard the maid's footsteps approach the front door, come to a stop, and her voice, without a word being spoken by the person who had rung, sorrowfully repeat:

"Poor Jeanne. My Poor Jeanne."

Jeanne was my grandfather's servant.

A moment's silence: the two women were kissing each other; tired of waiting, my father heard the sound of a cab vanishing into the dawn, and knew at once what the matter was. Jeanne gently pushed the door open, as though she was now in dread of all rooms.

"He's not dead, is he?" my father asked.

"They've taken him to hospital, sir."

My father has given me a description of the Reichbach grave-digger, up to his waist in the pit, looking up and listening, in the smell of the sun-warmed, rose-coloured sandstone, to one of my uncles saying: "Come along, Franz, hurry up. It's one of the family." We had about twenty cousins in the district, and the grave-digger bore a striking resemblance to my dead grandfather.

"I have heard a lot of nonsense talked about suicide," my father used to say, "but for a man who kills himself boldly I have never encountered any feeling but respect. Whether suicide is an act of courage or not is a question which concerns only those who have not killed themselves. For the others, there is a pact of silence; not one of us spoke of your grandfather otherwise than if he had died of a blood-clot."

Most of my uncles and great-uncles had not met for years. They had been kept apart less by circumstances than by the conflict between those of them who accepted German domination and those who rejected it—although this conflict had never got so far as an open rupture. Several of them now lived in France. They were all together at the home of Uncle Mathias, who helped my grandfather manage his factory. The only one who had not come was Great-uncle Walter. Was he really abroad for a few months? For fifteen years he had been estranged from his brother Dietrich, my grandfather, but however hard-hearted, however self-willed he was depicted, it was not in his nature to hear a grudge forever. Yet he was absent, and his absence increased the feeling of hostility that had always surrounded his name, that surrounded it still: my grandfather used to speak of him with more resentment—also with more insistence—than of all his other brothers, but he had appointed him (as he had appointed my father) as his legal executor.

My father did not know him. Unable to admit anyone, in his own family, who did not show towards him the obedience due to the tribal chief, Walter was not hated but was treated with that respect which the passion for authority creates when it has been exercised unremittingly for forty years. Having no children of his own, he had picked on one of my cousins and had developed an austere, formal affection for him: when the child was barely twelve, he would write him short notes every morning, full of injunctions that were like commands, and would insist on having an answer from him before he set off for school. At the age of twenty, after a dispute over some girl or other, my cousin left him. Uncle Walter, in spite of his wife's distress, had never answered his letters. This cousin, whom he had dreamt of making his heir, became an overseer. Walter never mentioned him, and his brothers discovered in his grief, of which they were well aware, so much warmth of heart that they were compelled to wonder that in other respects Walter had none.

It is true that if ever their brother proved too intolerable, they were all prepared to say: "With an affliction like his, it's a wonder he's no worse." All his photographs showed him standing, his crutches concealed by his long coat: both his legs were paralysed.

With Alsace foie-gras following the crayfish and trout at this funeral dinner, and raspberry brandy the Traminer wine, the reunion almost ended up as a festivity.

The millennia have not been long enough for man to learn how to look on death. The smell of fir-trees and resin which came through the summer windows, the thousand objects in polished wood, caused these childhoods spent in the family forestry business to harmonise with the memories and secrets of their past; and all were united in the tender respect which death allowed them to feel unreservedly for the rebel bourgeois laird whose baffling suicide seemed to crown his life with a secret.

Already old when, for a consideration, the Church had approved certain relaxations in the rules for Lent, my father had made a violent protest to the vicar, who was his protégé, for he was Mayor of Reichbach. (A fundamental factor: in this district, overlaid with traces of the "Holy Forest" of the Middle Ages, the boroughs still own vast tracts of common land, and Reichbach possessed ten thousand acres, which provided the best part of the municipal funds. My grandfather's professional qualifications were unchallenged.) "But Mr. Berger, is it proper for a mere priest to question the decisions of Rome?" "Then I shall go to Rome."

He had made the pilgrimage on foot. As chairman of various good works, he had had no difficulty in obtaining an audience of the Pope. He had found himself with about twenty of the faith in a room in the Vatican. He was not bashful, but the Pope was the Pope, and he was a Christian; they had all knelt down, the Holy Father had walked by, they had kissed his slipper, and they had been dismissed.

After re-crossing the Tiber, my grandfather, prey to

a holy indignation which covered the profane multitude of the fountains, the commonplace background of the pavementless streets, the ancient pillars, the tea-shops of plum-coloured plush, rushed off to pack up and punch down his bags, and left by the first express.

On his return, his Protestant friends believed he was ripe for conversion.

"One does not change one's religion at my age."

Thereafter, cut off from the Church but not from Christ, he attended mass every Sunday outside the building, standing in the midst of the nettles in one of the angles formed by the junction of the nave and the transept, following the service from memory, carefully listening at the window for the shrill sound of the handbell proclaiming the Elevation. Gradually he grew deaf and, afraid of not hearing, ended up by spending twenty minutes on his knees in the nettles of summer or the mud of winter. His enemies said he was no longer in his right mind, but it is not easy to dismiss unflinching determination; and for everyone this figure with his short white beard and frock-coat, kneeling in the mud underneath his umbrella, in the same spot, at the same time and for the same reason for so many years, presented less the spectacle of a crackpot than of a man of good sense. Alsace is alive to faith, and in those days she had good reason for being so to faithfulness.

It needed all his personal credit, however, all the success with which he managed his factory (people believe most readily in the madness of the unsuccessful) to make them accept the consequences of his Roman venture. When the lease between the Jewish community and the owner of the house in which it had set up its synagogue had expired, the owner refused point blank to renew it, and no one was willing to take his place as landlord. To the Municipal Council my grandfather suggested that they should let one of the Council buildings; he came up against strict opposition.

"Bear in mind, gentlemen, that this is unfair."

Steadfast silence, stubbornness of Alsace equal to his own. Although he was practically anti-semitic, he summoned the rabbi that very evening, put at his disposal free-of-charge a wing of that very house, beams jutting, tree-trunks echoing behind its huge doorway of Louis XVI iron-work, where my uncles were now finishing their feast.

It was the same story with the circus to which the Council had refused permission to camp on Reichbach territory: my grandfather gave it a home in the timber sheds which lay behind the house.

And my uncles, their fluted glasses and raspberry brandy in front of them, were in brotherly hysterics over the memory of the glorious night when they had all together set the animals free and when, after Mathias had opened the splendid, secretly oiled door, the older ones had ridden out, one on the wise old ass, another on the circus pony, another on the camel and my father on the elephant. Regardless of the screams of their new masters, the animals had made off into the woods; the whole village had to be mobilised to bring the mayor back his children who were now plastered with summonses.

Not only that, but when the next circus came through, he had locked the children up and granted the same hospitality.

In the huge house, where a whole East India Company gathering slept in the summer-shuttered rooms to the cricket-sound of the sawmill, one of the circuses had left behind a green macaw. My grandfather had taught it three words: "Do your duty." Should one of the children be punished, it seemed that Casimir—the parrot—could divine what had happened; as soon as the child came within range of the perch, the macaw would beat its wings: "Do your du-ooty! Do your du-ooty!" and the child would run off for some parsley, which is poison for parrots. This one ate it, grew fat on it, and ended up by loving it.

How many summer evenings had this company fallen asleep to the muted sound of the saws and the smell of the warm wood, with Jews golden as Rembrandt's creeping furtively past, clowns harnessing bears, a kangaroo in flight across the mountainous stacks of tree-trunks? Ever since my grandfather's body had been brought back there, the macaw, which was still alive, would leave its perch and flutter clumsily through the darkened rooms screeching into the void as if embodying the spirit of the dead man: "Do your du-oo-ooty."

My grandfather had made no mistake: his heir, the inheritor of his lordly despotism, was indeed the absentee, his brother Walter. Business men and merchants themselves, all my uncles looked up to him as a great professor. (Perhaps only my father commanded as much of their respect at the time.) After a fine career as an historian, which would have been brilliant had he not come from Alsace, he had founded those "Altenburg Discussion Groups" to which none of those who were now at Reichbach attending the funeral festival had been invited, and which were, in their view, of great social importance. He was a persistent and no doubt cunning organiser and had collected the necessary funds for the purchase of the historic priory of Altenburg, a few kilometres from Sainte-Odile. Every year he collected there some of his eminent colleagues, about fifteen intellectuals of every country, and the most gifted of his old pupils. Papers by Max Weber, Stefan George, Sorel, Durkheim, Freud were born of these discussions. Finally—and for my father this was not without its interest or importance—Walter had once been a friend of Nietzsche.

A strange character, what with the memory of Nietzsche and the actual table-talk: after Agadir he had dared to arrange a discussion on "Nations in the Service of the Intellect". But all his brothers (and still more all his nephews) recalled that when he was quite a child—it was between 1850 and 1860 when Alsace still belonged to France—he had answered his father's question about what he would do later in life with: "I shall work at the Académie Française." "What the devil will you do there?" "There'll be Mr. Victor Hugo, Mr. de Lamartine, Mr. Cuvier, Mr. de Balzac . . ." "And you?" "I shall be behind the lectern." "What the devil would you do behind the lectern?" "I? I should say to them: 'Begin all over again!' "

My father claimed that Altenburg was born of that old dream, never, alas, realised.

The following week he received a letter from Walter: the latter had just come home to Altenburg and was expecting him there.

My father was well aware that Walter was appreciative of fame in all its forms; and his own had been of consequence in some of the circles in which his uncle had connections, ever since a number of articles in magazines devoted to Eastern affairs—and a report which was still half-secret—had marked him out as the *éminence grise* of Enver Pasha.

A year earlier, in January 1913, everyone had thought that Turkey had been thrown out of Europe; with her army defeated and the Balkan forces only thirty kilometres from Constantinople, her government had, once again, sued for peace. Her conquerors were relying too openly on Russia for the Wilhelmstrasse to turn a blind eye.

Under the presidency of the Grand Vizier—a man of 90—the Cabinet was seeking a compromise. What else could it seek? Greece held the islands, the Allies had been in Chatalja for seven weeks. Officials and state servants had flooded into the secret council-chamber with their hands up like common lackeys at pistol-point and with kicks in the behind. In the midst of this hurly-burly of officers, Enver, at that time commanding the Tripoli army, had suddenly appeared in the huge doorway. At the third step he took towards him, the Minister for War fell to the ground clutching his stomach. Enver had put the compromise-experts into custody, thrown the text of the armistice terms and a few recalcitrants out of the window, and seized power with Talaat and Jemal. Then, when the quarrel between the Balkan allies at last broke out, he had re-formed the Turkish army in one month, assumed the offensive, and, after a forced march of eighty-four kilometres in one day, reached Adrianople. Constantinople was saved. The special correspondents had cabled to their papers, and the embassies to their governments, that the authority of the triumvirate would not last a month. It lasted, it organised, it was victorious.

In those days it was usual to look behind the backs of Moslem leaders for their European advisers.

2

My father was appointed to the rising university of Constantinople as soon as he had got his degree in oriental languages, and quickly won the fond respect of the young intellectuals there. This he owed both to the fervour and to the subject of his teaching: when he spoke about Nietzsche (his first course of lectures, in 1908, was entitled "The Philosophy of Action") the echo of the still almost occult voice of Zarathustra did much to amplify the taut eloquence of Professor Vincent Berger, which was all the more striking in Turkish in that it made use of slogans instead of the traditional arabesque style.

At that time my father was probably quite different from the man I remember; and yet, in spite of his drooping moustache, which was later clipped but which I recognised as the model of the one he grew in old age, his photographs of the period reveal a face closely approximating to the one I knew.

As a child, I loved to watch the wings of gliding gulls: I was more attracted by their double scythe-like blades than by the window of a cake-shop. One day I was with a group of fisherman standing round a dead frigate bird—perhaps it had been killed, perhaps it had died a natural death—which lay flattened on the pier at Bornholm: the stunted body of a hen between two huge, superb wings. For me my father's physical appearance has always been associated with the word "frigate": with the bird and even with the boat, which I cannot distinguish from a corvette and which I have probably never seen. Not only his face, which a draughtsman could not represent without each feature vaguely suggesting a claw, but also his slender, sinewy limbs, his delicate, knotted, fencer's hands, which reminded me of the firm articulation of those long wings still alive on either side of the dead bird; and above all the brisk, regal bearing of his tall, hunched body with its rather dangling arms. His commanding aspect came perhaps from his deep-set, light-blue eyes, which had a hard look —except when he used to watch me playing when I was a child. When old age made him long-sighted, he had only to put on his glasses for this sharp harpooner's face to become the face of an easy-going, absent-minded intellectual.

"Do you know what a shaman is?" one of my Russian friends once asked me.

"A Siberian medicine-man, isn't it?"

"Something else besides: Lenin was a great man, but he was not a shaman: Trotsky is less great, but he is a shaman. Pushkin, Robespierre, Goethe?—not at all shaman. But Dostoievsky, Mirabeau, Hölderlin, Poe: great shamans! There are little shamans: Heine. Napoleon was not a real shaman: he believed too much in things. Shamans are to be found among geniuses, and also, of course, among idiots. With us, in Russia, there are more shamans than in other countries. Well now, the strength and the weakness of Vincent Berger lies in his being a bit of a shaman."

Maybe. But it was the shaman that had said: "Bear in mind that a man's most effective weapon lies in reducing the curious side of his character to a minimum."

I failed to see the important side of his character which everyone always fails to see in his own people. But he taught me too much. I am too firmly convinced that a man's significance depends more on his achievements than on his secret qualities to care much about the secret qualities of those I love. The love of parents for their children is universal, and filial love is rare. But since I had a father I was happy, and sometimes proud, that it was he.

The German Ambassador in Constantinople had realised that, in his philosophy of action, action came before philosophy. This young man interested, amused and intrigued him all at once. When he had asked him his opinion of the Young Turk movement, after listening to what some chatterboxes had to say, my father had taken him aside: "With your permission, Your Excellency, a truce to this folly! Let's talk of matters over which we can have some control." Then he told the Ambassador what he did not know before—that the movement, which for several months had extended beyond the intellectual circles to attract the officer class, had begun substituting the technical study of revolution for democratic agitation.

"How would you organise a proper propaganda department in this establishment?" the Ambassador asked him one day, half sarcastically, half in earnest. My father did not misunderstand the question, nor the other his reply. A few months later, a propaganda service was in existence, my father being responsible for its organisation and management under the direct control of the Ambassador.

He distrusted even himself, and acted with greater caution than an internuncio. Out of propaganda, a mere device, he was bent on creating a means of political action. All the power was in the hands of Sultan Abdul Hamid who exercised it by means of the Porte—with viziers and government in a state of disintegration—and seemed to exercise it also through some other machinery, more powerful, more directly under his control. What was this other machinery, which had all the appearance of a huge police force, and above all what was its object?

Usually, in dictatorships, the policy of the dictator is well known and his personality little known; in this case the personality of the Sultan was fairly well known, but no one could make out his policy. He was said to be mad, and he certainly seemed so. Once when a bug was found in the bed he had selected (it was known that he never slept two nights running in the same room) he had suspected the bug of being poisoned and had dismissed a couple of officials. He granted audiences with his hand on his revolver, and his subjects had to keep their heads bowed —when one of them had stumbled and raised his head the Sultan had fired at once. In the palace the word "Turk" was used only as an insult; army commanders who were suspected of nationalism were sacked on the spot. The leading crook in Constantinople, appointed to the Admiralty by the cynical Sultan, had been sumptuously rewarded for destroying the fleet. The use of the words "Turkish fatherland" in the presence of the Caliph was punished by death.

Some of those who were connected with my father either by sympathy or by interest were in fairly close touch with Government House; by gradually piecing together the jig-saw of events he managed to unearth some intelligible reason for the "red Sultan's" anxiety.

This terrified ruler, whom the Turkish generals only reluctantly saw, received the principal pan-Islamic agents hospitably, and without a revolver; this idler, for whom the only tolerable things on earth were solitude, poetry and, best of all, police reports, himself drew up countless proclamations intended for the Moslems abroad; he communicated personally with the spiritual directors of Islam; this bankrupt sultan who had no money for his soldiers' boots was never short of it for the missions of his two hundred thousand agents. And for several years the name of the Turkish Sultan had been proclaimed in daily prayer from Fez to Kabul, and in all the mosques of India. If he had forbidden the word "fatherland", it was only because the Ottoman Empire, made up of twenty countries, would not oppose this new idea that was seeping in from the West. The Caliph's task had been to defend Allah; Allah now had to save the Empire by means of the Caliph. In the Wilhelmstrasse it was thought that the revived Caliphate would be able to launch the Holy War as soon as it was necessary, and immobilise the Moslem troops of England, France and Russia.

But as fast as my father discovered the extent and relative accuracy of the pan-Islamic machinery, he discovered also its incurable weakness. Clever enough to realise he was not responsible for carrying out his Ambassador's policy, he yet revealed to the latter that the worship revived by the Caliph outside Turkey would not produce political power for the Sultanate, that an alliance with infidel Germany would deprive the declaration of the Holy War of all its effect, and that the pan-Islamic agents, contrary to what the Sultan believed, were far from constituting a sufficiently powerful propaganda organ in Turkey to counteract that fact. He stressed the point that the Young Turk movement, which had been regarded (by Wilhelm II in particular) as democratic, full of idle talk and quite negligible, was now controlled by the old Russian terrorists of the Caucasus, was ready to revolt and would be successful; that political power would thus be placed in the hands of atheists. So that the Ambassador, compelled to avoid compromising himself but resolved to take action (he knew that Bülow did not share his Sovereign's

illusions), had made the head of his propaganda department a semi-official delegate to the Young Turks—a
delegate who could always be disowned.

At the beginning of July 1908 the revolt broke out in
Macedonia and the constitution was granted. The
European embassies now had to choose between revolu-
tion and the Sultan.

At the German Embassy—which had become far more
than an embassy with the teeming mission in charge of re-
organising the army—there was more heated partisanship
than anywhere else. The setbacks of Parliament multiplied;
and if some of the officials connected with the Young
Turk officers sympathised with the movement, the inclination of many others, including the Emperor, was towards
the Sultan: they saw that all power was vested in him.

"What does the propaganda section make of our
democrats?" the Naval Attaché had once asked rather
scornfully.

German politics roused no strong feeling in my father.
For him the social problem had never arisen. The victory
of German socialism seemed to him certain and desirable:
it would put an end to the tragedy of Alsace and destroy
the Junkers caste which he hated. So he was not sorry
to engage with his own weapons the man who had asked
him the question:

"The Young Turks are making mistake after mistake,
and will go on doing so for quite a time. *But*, apart from
them, there's nothing. Nothing. In the general decomposition of this country only one thing counts: the army. The
Young Turks are the only ones at the moment who are

capable first of maintaining it, then of developing it. Authority is all right, but power is better. Whoever governs will not be able to govern without it. Nothing else matters.

"An army alone cannot make a State. But a new factor has cropped up in the last six months: the Moslems of the Caucasus, trained by the revolutionaries of Russia, are gradually assuming considerable authority in the Young Turk committees. Without being forced to combat the general ideology of the movement, we can alter its cadres from top to bottom, replacing, as in every revolution, the assembly-men in it with committee-men—with dictatorship-men, if you like. What the Young Turk cadres, and even the masses, will always regard as being in their own interest, even as a fulfilment of their own ideas—never as a reaction—is a dictatorship exercised by men of the people, like Talaat and Jemal, or one of the officers who launched the revolution, such as Enver."

For weeks my father had been suggesting to the latter a radical change in the movement: the creation, among the experienced revolutionaries, of cadres chosen exclusively for their discipline and toughness, trained in street-fighting. And for weeks he had been despatching via Egypt—Germany not intending to be compromised in any way—machine guns of the latest type to the Young Turks.

When the counter-revolution, organised by the Sultan's agents, had been crushed in Constantinople by the Young Turk army of Macedonia, as my father had foreseen, the Ambassador pointed out to him—with Abdul Hamid deposed and replaced by the ghostly Mohammed V, and

43

with the power of Parliament definitely restored—that
such talk was hardly in keeping with his office; that it was
improper to publicise a policy (the change in the cadres)
which was excellent only in so far as it remained secret.
He was all the more distressed because unable to deny it.
He had let himself be carried away; lack of caution was his
chief fault, the reverse of the coin whose obverse was
"shamanism". The Embassy, for whom a go-between
with a clandestine organisation had been essential, had
no wish for anybody between itself and the Turkish
Ministry of Foreign Affairs.

Angry, but not surprised—the game had been played
according to the rules—he waited.

The influence which he no longer possessed with the
Germans he still possessed with the Turks, who had taken
what Germany had been giving them. Moreover, he main-
tained his position in the Embassy; in theory, the propaganda department had not ceased to exist. He had formed
a close friendship with Enver; his proposals gave a shape
to that young colonel's still confused ideology. The latter
was known to the Germans, for he had done his military
training in the Prussian Guard, had been Military Attaché
at Berlin; his romantic zest used to cause them some mis-
giving, often annoyed them. It was suited to the tempera-
ment of my father, who managed to get himself attached
to him when, on Italy's declaration of war on Turkey,
Enver was promoted to General and given command of
the Tripoli army.

When they reached the coast of Sirte in a smuggling
vessel towards the end of 1910, the Itàlians were holding

all the large harbours. Very thin on the ground, the Turkish troops were scattered from the Egyptian frontier to the Tunisian. No hope of reinforcements from Constantinople; and no question of tackling the Italian navy with the old tubs whose rusty guns Abdul Hamid had inspected with a sneer.

The talent which my father had shown for interpreting a complex situation, for finding the right bit of string to pull in order to unravel the ball, this time worked wonders. Also, perhaps, the fact of his not being a professional soldier: the catastrophic state of the army had floored Enver at first. Here, at last, was his chance: the most effective weapon at this juncture, the secret service, was the one he knew best.

The head of the military and religious order of the Libyan Desert, the Grand Senussi, offered to put his native troops at Enver's disposal. They were far too weak to be matched against Graziani's army. My father's proposal was to mobilise the tribes of the Libyan Desert with the help of the Senussi, and to try to paralyse the Italians by modern guerrilla action without giving battle.

The Italians were going to make an attempt to penetrate into the interior: the organisation of an intelligence service was therefore the most urgent task. My father was sufficiently conversant with the service of the German Embassy at Constantinople, and also with the Turkish, to find no difficulty in carrying out this task with the help of a dozen Turkish specialists trained in Germany. He needed only senior cadres: the Senussi would provide the junior agents by the hundred, either by selecting them

from their own ranks, or by recruiting them. In contrast
with Christians, every Moslem, however little he was paid,
was an agent. My father knew he could still expect sub-
stantial help from Germany: "The evacuation of Cyrenaica
would be suicide," Von der Goltz had declared. But
clandestine help is, by definition, limited. At any rate,
he at once got some money—which Enver had been
expecting from Constantinople for a long time—and
some excellent machine-guns.

With these Enver equipped the Turkish military
vehicles and supplemented them with others yielded by
a dozen apparently pointless raids, and by means of
them supported the extremely mobile squadrons of
cavalry and native troops which he kept in hiding near
each of the ports. The water points were too few and
far between (the Turks would have poisoned them anyway) for a whole Italian army to venture into the desert.
Graziani flung in five columns: all five were wiped out.

As my father had hoped, these minor victories,
exaggerated by the Senussi agents, united the tribes, who
were in any case well paid. The Italians were masters
of the sea but were not in control of the tracks in Southern
Tunisia nor those in Southern Egypt. From Turkey—
and from Germany—arms and munitions were arriving
in sufficient quantities for the picked troops; for the
rest, the native workshops, when properly organised
(the nomads are good armourers), were sufficient. A
price was put on Enver's head and on my father's;
the Italians referred to the latter by the name which
the Arabs had given him: "Hatchet Face."

Enver's qualities and defects, his dash, his toughness, his romantic temper, his charm, all made an impression on the lords of the sands: in three months the desert was his to command. By adding to his personal influence the credit of being engaged to one of the Caliph's daughters, he accomplished the feat of imposing discipline on the nomadic hordes, and out of those that were not intended for desert piracy he succeeded in building a regular army strong enough, in conjunction with the remnants of the Turkish garrisons, to lay siege to Derna.

He was hardly likely to succeed in taking the town; but the Italians, who had started out as conquerors, were now the beleaguered.

This lasted until the Balkan menace, towards the end of the year, forced Constantinople to come to terms with the Italians. No sooner had the peace been signed than the entire Balkans fell on Turkey. To the surprise of the experts, the Turkish army, although reorganised by the Germans, was mopped up in a fortnight.

With negligible resources, with no hope of victory, Enver had held Graziani in check for nearly a year. He became a hero. My father, obeying an urgent summons to Constantinople, arrived there as Enver's envoy to the Germans rather than as his German adviser. The Young Turks were nothing more than an opposition party. The Grand Vizier, head of a Cabinet composed of Abdul Hamid's old ministers, was born in 1820.

"What action do you think we can take?" Bülow's special envoy asked him.

"It's too late to take action through any *thing*; we can only take action through some *one*, and that someone can only be Enver. They say the army has been reduced to dust. That's not his opinion. Nor is it General von der Goltz's, nor mine. The point is to release the army from the stupid shackles with which the ministers have hobbled it. The soldiers are brave; the cadres organised by our mission are good. There's no need to rebuild it, but only to destroy what is destroying it. The Balkan army is not Moltke's, as far as I know, and there is serious dissent in its ranks."

"What are Enver Pasha's intentions . . . his plans?"

"To return as soon as possible, and to seize power."

"Although the Government is not exactly strong, I . . ."

"We shall seize power."

At the word "we", the envoy pricked up his ears.

"On what conditions does Enver Pasha propose a settlement with the Balkans?"

"We can only come to terms through victory; you know that as well as I do. First, victory: and then technicians and equipment as soon as possible. Secondly, the old satellite provinces of Europe hardly matter: Enver's not interested in them, and therefore . . ."

"What the hell is he interested in, then?"

"Ottomanism, the union of all Turks throughout Central Asia from Adrianople to the Chinese oases on the Silk Trade Route. Nations are born, here as much as anywhere else; we shall not prevent the existence of Greece or Serbia. The point is to go ahead; then, once

48

an acceptable peace has ensured us the Turkish provinces
of Europe, to let our old Christian provinces go to hell
and, instead of dreaming of a ridiculous Republic of
Constantinople, to put in its place the Young Turk
Empire, with Samarkand as the capital."

The envoy was quite sharp and quite shrewd; but his
habit of trying to find some hidden meaning in everything he heard retarded his intelligence when confronted
with those who had nothing to hide. This man he was
listening to, who seemed too young for the part he
had played (although the one he was now playing was not
lacking in importance), this man whose abrupt way of
talking was in keeping with his fine, bony face and nervous
hands, intrigued him in the same way that he had intrigued
the Ambassador.

He had heard my father described as a clear-minded
man, and also as an adventurer. Romantic? Certainly;
but no romantic displayed such intellectual precision,
or such mastery of the means at his disposal; besides,
although my father was not indifferent to power he cared
nothing for money. And is there not something romantic
about every great ambition? The envoy thought, however, that for a man of great ambition my father talked
too fast and too much.

"How is it," he asked, "that you feel so . . . so
personally interested in Ottomanism? Enthusiastic about
it, if I may say so."

What the origin of this enthusiasm was, my father had
hardly considered. It was mixed up with the need to get
away from Europe, the lure of history, the fanatical

desire to leave some scar on the face of the earth, the attraction of a scheme to which he had contributed not a few of the finer points, the comradeship of war, friendship.

"Activity which is fostered by dreams instead of being blighted by them is hard to find," he said, half in jest. Then, with a broader grin: "What have you got to offer me that's better?"

The envoy brushed the question aside with his hand, as if for the sake of caution, with a polite, professional gesture. He might perhaps have answered "Germany", my father thought. But—apart from Alsace—his only fellow-feeling was for those he had chosen. Besides, in the service of a great power he would only have been an executive; with Enver he was more than that. And what perhaps disturbed the envoy still more, although he was only vaguely conscious of it, was the fact that my father could now feel completely useful and enthusiastic only in the service of something he had himself conceived or helped to conceive.

The argument of "this rather eccentric but far from unpractical young man" had attracted Bülow's attention: the eventual claim to Russian Turkestan would make Russo-Turkish antagonism more violent than ever. Berlin knew that in the event of a European war Turkey would do her utmost to remain neutral. But if Jamal were even to suggest an alliance with England and France, Russia, intent on preventing it, would throw her weight into the scales to have his proposal rejected; and Turkey would thus be forced into an alliance with Germany.

When Enver returned—just in time—from Tripoli, everything was ready.

With the ministers ejected under a battering of truncheons, the Turkish army, for the first time since the Battle of Plevna, now had a war leader.

Enver's youth and dash made the same impression on it as Bonaparte's had made on the Italian army. The Pasha was less of a big white chief, but he had better support: if he were defeated Germany could no longer rely on Turkey. My father had been right in stating that it was not so much a question of rebuilding the army as of crushing what was paralysing it. A single offensive, no more, saved Constantinople; but, as soon as a second one had relieved Adrianople, Russia advised the Balkans to come to terms; in May the peace was signed. Turkey was to remain in Europe.

My father knew only too well that from then on his close connection with Enver would not be regarded without suspicion by the German Embassy, unless that connection was exploited exclusively in its service. But he felt himself more bound to Enver than to it; embassies were not what he loved more than anything else in the world. At that time he used to say with reckless irony: "For a man who has the choice, his country is the country where the largest clouds are gathering." Besides, certain newspapers had begun to build him up as the *éminence grise* behind the victory, and he was quite aware that one day Enver would resent this: he knew how conceited he was. He could perhaps have found some means of destroying the mythical person he was growing into, had he been compelled. But he had no wish to do so. His reputation was flattering. What was more important, he enjoyed it.

No sooner was the peace assured than his thirst for Ottomanism became the Generalissimo's main obsession. Contact had to be established with the Turks of Central Asia, a direct link forged with the Kurds, the emirs of Bokhara and Afghanistan, the khans of Russian Turkestan. "Afghanistan first of all," the German Ambassador suggested. It was closer to India. And everyone considered my father the obvious man for the job: the Germans, Enver—and my father himself.

3

Two months later he was at Ghazni. Arriving via India, he had stayed as short a time as possible at Kabul, which was full of English agents.

Afghanistan did not exist. The Emir was only Emir of Kabul. He was having the telephone installed and connecting the town to India with a telegraph line; but thirty miles away the primitive world of Islam began. Every khan paid tribute if he was weak, exacted it if he was strong. And nothing united the shifting or static dust that stretched from Persia to Samarkand except the law of the Koran.

From steppe to steppe, my father, whose small, pointed beard now gave him the angular appearance of a Persian prince, conferred with khans who looked like crows, like corpulent cooks, like vultures. Almost all of them had heard of Enver, the Moslem general who had defeated the Christians; for the rest, their answers remained flatteringly vague. And my father went farther on, met fresh khans, some of them like the patrician warriors of the hegira, others who would have made perfect carpet-sellers but for their lack of physical cowardice. He met with the same meticulously ambiguous speeches, the same uneasiness, the same nothingness. And coming down from the Pamir, where lost camels bleat across the mist, coming back from the sands of the South where, in the thorn bushes, crickets larger than crayfish raise the antennae on their knight's helms at the sound of a caravan passing, he reached some bone-coloured town. Under the gateway made of clay and bristling with beams, horsemen in rags sat dreaming, their legs stretched out on their stirrups; at the foot of buildings veiled like women, horses' skulls and scaly fish-bones glittered in the dust of the windowless streets. Out of doors, not a leaf; indoors, not a stick of furniture: the walls, the sky, and God.

"After three years," a caravan driver had told him, "you forget the desert is empty."

He was now reminded of the desert; and of the lords of the desert. In the Senussi oases, the bareness of the soul had been still more pronounced, but it was in keeping with the blazing presence of God, with war, with the structure of united Islam. Here, the God of the Burning Bush was mere ritual; at the end of every eighteen-course feast of rice, it seemed that the tribe was about to

53

split up, to fall into dust. In Tripoli my father had acted; here he talked.

Suffering from an increasingly painful bout of dysentery and in a brooding frame of mind, he resumed his journey along the Hindu Kush, through thistles large as artichokes. On the other side of the mountains was India, her salmon-coloured towns decorated like festival sweetmeats, where monkeys crossed the streets in pensive herds to keep in the shade; and the sea . . . Oh for the green of Europe! Trains whistling in the night, the rattle and clatter of late cabs . . .

One day as he was strolling through the bazaar at Ghazni, a madman—with the intuition that madmen sometimes have, this one perhaps guessed that my father was not a Turk—fell on him and beat him up. There was no question of hitting back: Moslem deference to madness is sustained to the full in Central Asia. And the man would have killed him, if only he had found some larger stones.

My father went back to his house in a rage, severed and somehow released from a spell: suddenly, abruptly, he realised the truth: Ottomanism, the incentive to the new Turkish aspirations which had perhaps saved Constantinople, simply did not exist.

He had taken months to realise this.

The existence of Ottomanism had seemed so clear to him that he had never questioned it. Just as countless zealous Christians before Luther had come to Rome without noticing the corruption there; just as the anglophile French of the eighteenth century came back from London without having noticed the power of the aristocracy staring them in the face, so had he failed, during all these months, to grasp, assess and compare the facts, except in terms of the Ottoman myth. One is as easily blinded by a country which gives birth to a myth in which one believes as by a woman one loves.

Had the strange accident that had set him free taken place at the opportune moment when the myth, for want of blood, was on the point of collapse? He felt neither more friendly nor more hostile towards the Afghans, and considered he had only himself to blame. Yet he realised that what had set him free was humiliation.

He now knew what one could expect from these people. They would willingly fight for Enver, the victorious general who had become the Caliph's son-in-law; that is, on condition he paid them well and the risk was not too great (they would have thought twice about fighting against England). In the name of Ottomanism? Certainly. Islam would have been enough. Besides, wherever my father had made his mark, it was thanks to the old pan-Islamic agents of Abdul Hamid. The skeleton of Islam was the only framework supporting these people who were sleep-walking among their ruins, between the nakedness of the mountains and the solemn tremor of the white sky.

There remained the Turkomans and the Sartes of the Russian steppes. Their reaction would be the same, unless they thought—mistakenly—that their hour of liberation was at hand.

For Enver, Ottomanism was a necessary factor, and

there could be no question of its not existing: even a
report from my father would not alter the fact: if the
latter had seen no sign of Ottomanism, it was simply
that he was blind. But the quality of loyalty was all the
stronger in him for being part of his natural character
and also of his romantic attitude. Although he was certain
of courting disaster, perhaps, in his heart of hearts,
he still hoped to convince Enver. He merely notified him
of his return: he was relying more on his powers of
persuasion than on his written reports, and illness had
laid him low the moment he had lost all faith in the
mission with which he had been entrusted. He waited
another month for the return of the emissaries who had
been sent to the Russian frontier and to Bokhara,
finally reached Peshawar with a fever which turned the
Hindu houses into pink spinning-tops, and at Karachi
found a cargo vessel from which he could not disembark
en route.

His plan was to spend a few weeks at Reichbach, or
in a nursing-home in Strasbourg, and from there go back
to Constantinople.

Enver was in Jaffa when the ship reached Suez;
feeling worried and impatient, he cabled to my father
and came to see him when the ship put in at Port Said.

Their conversation was a long one. Enver was a
gambler; my father was depriving him of his trump card,
and the General held it against him not so much because
he believed that my father was mistaken but because he
was afraid that he was not mistaken at all. Enver had a
fanatic faith in his luck, which had up to now served

him well; overcoming all obstacles, going ahead whatever the result, had, he believed, been the very source of all his achievements.

"When we launched the revolt in Macedonia, do you know how many of us there were in the plot? Three hundred! If Ottomanism is not yet conscious of itself, it's up to us to make it so."

Throughout the conversation he suggested to my father that illness had warped his judgement: if only my father believed it, then he, Enver, could believe it as well.

"Send another of your collaborators," my father said, offering the General a ray of hope. This discussion seemed pointless. Having been seriously ill at Ghazni, he had contributed to a mistake which had made great demands on himself; but with his health restored his hate returned: as though he had been deceived, not by himself, but by that false, idiotic Central Asia which rejected its own destiny, and by all those who had shared in his belief.

"I should have sent a Moslem in the first place," said Enver.

He bade my father a friendly farewell and was particularly solicitous about his health; but my father knew that something important between them had been lost forever.

By the time he got to Marseilles—having already shaved off his Persian beard—he was, if not quite recovered, at least on his feet again.

The landing formalities were not over until six in the evening; the Strasbourg express left in the morning.

My father took a cab and asked to be driven to a hotel in the Vieux Port. He had been out of Europe for six years.

Through the smiling blue haze, panama and straw hats, fine-checked trousers and strange female shapes glided past houses that had still a familiar look. The rush hour from offices and shops had not yet started; there were many more women in the streets than men.

My father remembered puff sleeves, chokers and bell-shaped skirts; and those enormous tea-cosies in embroidered muslin had been replaced by open-necked odalisques with exaggerated curves, whose hobbled steps suggested the crippled feet of Chinese women. In all this crowd, now quite a fashionable one,—he was nearing the Canebière—not a single face with an expression on it; the toques which were worn low on the brow in place of the former huge hats perched high on the head concealed everyone's eyes. No oriental woman wears a hat. And the intimacy of these women in their holiday dresses gave every face he could see the blank, fixed look of madmen's faces.

Up in his room, he rubbed himself down with a horse-hair glove to get rid of his nausea; through the open window behind the closed shutters came the hubbub of the summer-time Canebière, the cries of the news-paper-sellers, the metallic din of the trams—and strange tunes which were a cross between a waltz and a gypsy ballad, like the songs of a procession winding past, stopping and starting up again: he had never heard a tango.

He dressed quickly. In Afghanistan, how many times had he dreamt of the first thing he wanted to see again! The smell of train-smoke, asphalt in the sun, cafés at night, chimneys under a grey sky, bathrooms! After several months of Central Asia, whether asleep or listening to the endless trot of camels and Afghan horses, he used to dream of hoardings chequered with advertisements, of inexhaustible museums lined with paintings right up to the roof, as in the Dutch canvases depicting art-dealers' shops. But what he was now approaching as he almost raced downstairs, he had never thought of: that was the shop-windows.

Some of them he still recognised: chemists', antique-dealers', butchers', grocers', greengrocers' (but how red the meat was, how small and insipid the peaches!). Others puzzled him for a little: pedicurists', orthopaedists', flowershops, corset-shops, a hairdresser's with a notice he had never seen before: "chi-chi chignons"—a shop with funeral wreaths. Large mirrors reflected the ladies looking into them. My father now had time to scrutinize these ladies and was startled by their waddling gait, the immodesty of these clinging dresses which he had never seen in Europe and which Asia has never known. And yet the absence of the Moslem veil, the exposed faces, gave Europe a touching innocence. What stamped these faces was not nakedness, but work, worry, laughter—life. Unveiled.

"... the most ordinary things, streets, dogs ..." When would these words stop buzzing in his brain? The French papers were full of the trial of the anarchists whom they called "motorised bandits"; one of them had answered the doctors' interrogation with: "The identity of the victim is of no importance! But afterwards, something unforeseen happens: everything is different, the most ordinary things, streets, for instance, dogs. . . ."

The shedding of blood has power to disrupt for a moment the state of overpowering apathy that enables us to live; my father felt this type of shock in the very depths of his being. Not so much through what he was discovering anew as through what he was recognising again—through the once familiar species crowding round him at night in the Vieux Port, with its walking-sticks, its whiskered puppets, its tangoes and its warships.

Feeling like a castaway on the bank of either nothing-ness or eternity, he looked at its troubled waters—as divorced from it as from those who had passed by, with their forgotten sufferings and lost legends, in the streets of the early Bactrian and Babylonian dynasties, or in the oases overlooked by the Towers of Silence. Through the strains of music and the smell of warm bread, housewives were hurrying along, shopping-bags on their arms; a paint-shop put up its multicoloured shutters on which a last sunbeam lingered; a liner's siren wailed; inside a narrow shop deep in shadow, a shop assistant with a cap on his head was lifting a tailor's dummy on to his back— on earth, towards the end of the second millennium of the Christian era. . . .

He had once ardently awaited first communion and stopped the Reichbach vicar, who had the Host in his hand, to tell him of a sin which he had forgotten to confess the previous day. ("It's nothing, Vincent, my boy: three acts of contrition and three "Ave Marias. . . ."); instead of something startling, he had found only what he expected. This evening he felt released, as he had felt then—with a rapturous liberty which was indistinguishable from licence.

Five days after his return to Reichbach, his father killed himself. It was as though he had been waiting for him, either to see him again or else to be assured that his last wishes would be fulfilled.

II

I

THE library at Altenburg was admirable. A central pillar supported the high vaulted Romanesque ceiling where the bookshelves disappeared into the shadows, for the room was lit only by electric lamps placed at eye level. Darkness came in through a huge stained-glass window. Here and there were Gothic sculptures, photographs of Tolstoy and Nietzsche, a show-case containing the latter's letters to Uncle Walter, a portrait of Montaigne, the masks of Pascal and Beethoven (such family men, my father thought). In a deep recess his uncle sat waiting for him behind a desk that looked like a kitchen-table, purposely set apart—resting on a wooden stand one step high, which allowed him to tower above anyone he was talking to. In like manner, in a proudly humble cell, did Philip II turn his nose up at the imposing Escurial.

My father had seen Walter on the platform when the train stopped: if he did not know him, he knew his crutches. His uncle watched him approach, very erect, with two disciples by him, in the strange statuesque pose he adopted to screen his infirmity; a high collar and a narrow black tie were visible under the light Byronic cloak which concealed his knees; gold-rimmed spectacles rested on his broken Michelangelo nose—Michelangelo at the end of a long university career. His grand-style greeting had immediately been followed by:

"We get up at eight."

To my father's surprise, they had set out on foot. The disciples walked behind; the frowning ranks of fir-trees under a sky in which cotton-wool clouds were blown along on the breeze of that poor summer. The horses' hooves and the muffled squeak of the carriage following behind fitted in with the silent progress of the rubber-tipped crutches. Four hundred yards in front of them, where the dark sides of the valley converged, the priory at last came into sight, lovely in a harsh and heavy way. Propped up on his left crutch, Walter had pointed with his right hand:

"There it is." Then, modestly: "A barn, just a barn." How would he describe a castle! my father wondered.

"It's a barn," Walter had repeated, disregarding any comment. And they had finally got into the carriage.

Walter looked at the badly lit paintings and the rows of books in the shadows, as if he was expecting this cloister of the mind to put my father in a state of grace. The light shone on his face from below, accentuating its rough-cast features. He had put on his glasses, and this low light, bringing his face into relief, made it materialise as the face of his dead brother. Here was the man whom my father had wanted as his legal executor, after fifteen years' estrangement—and the magazines mentioning the part my father had played in Turkey had only been bought in order to be sent on to him.

"I was very fond of Dietrich," said Walter in the same tone he would have used for bestowing an honour, but with a hint of emotion.

His voice, like his face, had some hollow quality—as though he were afraid of committing himself by talking, or as though what he was going to say had barely taken his mind off his own thoughts. Yet he pursued his enquiry:

"He had made up some poison, they tell me, in case the veronal had . . . no effect?"

"On the bedside table there was a small bottle of strychnine. But his revolver was on the pillow as well, with the safety-catch off."

Standing every week, for so many years, at the same time, in the same place outside the church . . .

Walter nearly began to speak, stopped, finally made up his mind:

"Are you in a position to enlighten me—I merely say 'enlighten'—as to the reasons which could have . . . driven Dietrich to this . . . misadventure?"

"No. In fact I should say: 'on the contrary.' Two days before his death we had dinner together; just by chance, we talked about Napoleon. He asked me rather sarcastically: 'If you could choose another life, what sort would you choose?' 'What sort would you?' He thought it

over for quite a time and suddenly said, quite seriously:
'Well, you know, *whatever happens*, if I had to live another
life again, I should want none other than Dietrich
Berger's.' "

"I should want none other than Dietrich Berger's,"
Walter repeated half aloud.

"It's possible for a man to go on caring deeply—
fanatically—about himself, even when he has already
detached himself from life."

From outside, on the wings of the rainy evening,
came the crazy shrieks of hens. Walter stretched his hand
out towards my father to ask:

"And you have no reason to think that during the
following day something. . . ."

"Suicide was implied by his 'whatever happens'."

"Nevertheless, you didn't imagine anything?—I merely
say: 'imagine'."

He was saying: 'imagine'; merely 'imagine', that's
all; nothing more than 'imagine'.

"I was convinced that those who talk about suicide
never kill themselves."

The one man on earth, my father reflected bitterly,
to whom my few moments of success brought the most
joy or pride.

Walter muttered, as though searching his memory,
the stiffness of his lips accentuated by the low light:

"Yet it so happens that death can be recognised,
when it has struck several times."

"I had never seen anyone die whom I cared about."

"But these Balkans . . . hot-blooded, violent . . ."

"I'm back from Central Asia. For Moslems, life is a random chapter in the destiny of the universe; they never commit suicide. I've seen lots of them die, it's true, in Tripoli. But the ones I saw dying were not friends of mine."

Outside, the raindrops pattered on to the flat spindle-tree leaves, as though on to paper; at regular intervals a heavier drop, falling from some drainpipe, splashed down.

"As a child," said Walter, half aloud, "I was terribly frightened of death. Every year that has brought me closer to it has increased my indifference to it. 'The evening of life brings with it its lamp'; Joubert, I believe, said that."

My father did not answer. He was sure Walter was lying: he could detect his fear welling up.

"Why," asked the latter, "did Dietrich want to have a church funeral? It's odd—I merely say: 'odd'—and not in keeping with suicide. He knew that the Church does not allow suicides a religious burial except in so far as it admits their . . . irresponsibility."

He seemed to resent the decision with which his brother had died—and, at the same time, to be proud of it.

My father hesitated, then went on:

"I believe what he went through was extremely painful. You know the will was sealed. The words: 'My express wish is to have a religious burial' were written on a loose sheet placed on the table where the strychnine was; but what he had written at first was: 'My express wish is not to have a religious burial.' It was only afterwards

66

he crossed out the negative and scribbled over it several times. He probably didn't have enough strength left to tear the paper up and begin again."

"Fear?" Walter suggested.

"Or the end of the struggle: surrender."

"But anyway, how can we ever tell? Fundamentally speaking, man is what he hides."

Walter hunched his shoulders and brought his old hands together, like a child making a mud pie:

"A wretched little pile of secrets . . ."

"Man is what he achieves," my father answered, almost savagely. He was constitutionally opposed to what he called "the secret-theory", which he spoke of as he would speak of pick-pocketing. Even supposing there was a "cause" for my grandfather's suicide, that cause, whether it was the most commonplace or the most tragic secret, was less significant than the strychnine and the revolver—than the decision with which he had *chosen* death, a death that was like his life.

"In the realm of secrets," he went on, in a more subdued tone of voice, "men achieve equality a little too easily."

"Of course, you, I believe, are what is called a man of action."

"It isn't action that has made me understand that 'fundamentally speaking', as you put it, man is more than his secrets."

He remembered the bed in the dead man's room, rumpled by the hospital orderlies who had just removed the body, and timidly made up by Jeanne, with the hollow in it like the hollows that sleepers always make; the electric light was still on, as if no one—not even himself—dared to scare death away by drawing the curtains. In the half-open wardrobe stood a little Christmas tree, with so many tiny candles. An ashtray lay on the bedside table; inside it were three cigarette-ends; my grandfather had been smoking, either before taking the veronal or before falling asleep. An ant was scuttling along the rim of the ashtray. It continued on a straight course, then climbed on to the revolver lying there. Apart from a motor-horn in the distance and the clip-clop of a cab in the street, my father could hear nothing but the feeble sound of the travelling-clock which was still going. Mechanical and alive like this ticking, the insect social order was pullulating over the face of the earth, below the mysterious liberty of man. Death was in the room, in the disturbing light of electric bulbs when daylight is visible through the curtains, and in the vague traces left behind by the men who remove bodies; from the living world outside came the regular hooting of the motor horn, the diminishing sound of the horses' hoofs, early morning birdsong, men's voices—muffled, unintelligible. At this moment donkey caravans were making their way towards Kabul, towards Samarkand, their rattle and clatter drowned in the lassitude of Islam.

The human adventure, the world. And all of it, like his father's fulfilled destiny, could have been other than it was. He felt himself gradually possessed by an unknown sensation, as he had once been at night in the highlands of Asia by the divine presence, while the little desert owls fluttered their velvet wings in the silence around him. It was the same agonising sense of freedom, only far more pronounced, that he had felt that evening at Marseilles while watching the shadows glide through the rarified atmosphere of cigarettes and absinthe—when Europe had seemed so unfamiliar as he watched it and all the strange people in it, just as, released from the bonds of time, he would have watched an hour of the distant past slip slowly by. In the same way, he now felt the whole of his life was disordered; and suddenly he felt delivered from it—strangely unfamiliar with the world and astonished by it, as he had been by that street where the people of his rediscovered country went gliding across the green grass.

He had finally drawn the curtains. On the other side of the classical spirals of the huge iron doorway, the leaves were the bright green of early summer; a little further down the darker foliage began, culminating in the ranks of near-black fir-trees. He realised that he had been picturing all this vegetation as purple-coloured.

Like a man's fate, the whole of life was an adventure. He looked at the infinite repetitions of this commonplace countryside, listened to the prolonged rustlings of Reichbach as it came to life, just as in his youth he used to gaze beyond the constellations at smaller and smaller stars until his sight failed. And the mere presence of the people passing hastily by in the morning sunshine, as alike and as different as leaves, seemed to yield a secret that did not spring only from the death which still lurked behind him, a secret that was far less the secret of death than of life—a secret that would have been just as impressive if man had been immortal.

"I have known that sensation," said Walter. "And I sometimes feel I shall experience it again, when I am old . . ."

My father looked at this man of seventy-five who said: "when I am old". Walter returned his gaze, raised his hand:

"They tell me you once devoted one of the courses you gave to those . . . Turks was it? to my friend Friedrich Nietzsche. I was in Turin— just by chance, in Turin— when I heard he had just gone out of his mind. I hadn't seen him; I had just arrived. Overbeck, who had been notified, came dashing down, if I may say so, from Basle to see me: he had to take the poor fellow away at once, and he didn't even have enough money for the tickets. As usual. You . . . you know Nietzsche's face," (Walter pointed to a picture behind him) "but no photograph can convey his expression; it was as sweet as a woman's, in spite of his . . . bogy-man moustache. That expression had gone."

He continued to keep his head still, his voice low, as though he was speaking not to my father, but to the books and the famous photographs in the shadows, as though no one who listened to him was completely worthy of understanding him; or rather (my father's impression was growing more definite as he listened to him) as though the listeners who did understand what he was saying belonged to another epoch; as though nowadays no one was willing to understand; as though he was only speaking out of politeness, boredom and a sense of duty. In his whole manner there was the same haughty modesty that was expressed in his small, raised writing-desk.

"When Overbeck in his distress cried 'Friedrich!' the poor fellow embraced him and, immediately afterwards, absent-mindedly asked: 'Have you ever heard of Friedrich Nietzsche?' Overbeck stretched his hand out awkwardly. 'Have I? No, I . . . I'm a silly chap.'"

Walter's raised hand imitated Overbeck's. My father liked Nietzsche more than any other writer. Not for his doctrine but for the matchless liberality of spirit that he found in him. He listened, ill at ease, spellbound.

"Then Friedrich talked about the ceremonies that were being arranged for him. Well . . . we took him away. Luckily we had met a friend of Overbeck's, a . . . dentist, who was used to madmen. I hadn't much money on me; we had to take third-class tickets; it couldn't be helped. It was a long journey in those days from Turin to Basle. The train was more or less full of poor people, Italian workmen. His landlady had told us Friedrich was subject to violent fits. We managed to find three seats. I stood in the corridor, Overbeck sat on Friedrich's left; Miescher, the dentist, on his right; next to him was a peasant girl. She looked like Overbeck, the same old granny's face. A hen kept poking its head out of her basket; the girl kept shoving it in again. It was enough to drive one mad—yes, mad! What could it have been

like for a . . . a sick man? I thought something frightful
might happen.

"The train entered the St. Gothard tunnel, which had
just been completed. In those days it took thirty-five
minutes to go through—thirty-five minutes—and the
carriages, the third-class ones at any rate, had no lighting.
Swaying about in the dark, the smell of soot, the feeling
that the journey would never end . . . In spite of the noise
of the train on the metals, I could hear the hen's beak
pecking at the wicker-work, and I was on tenterhooks.
Supposing a crisis occurred in this darkness?"

Except for his lips, which were only just moving,
the whole of his face remained perfectly still in the
dramatic lighting; but his voice, punctuated by the
raindrops falling from the tiles, was shaking with the
scorn that is to be found in certain forms of pity.

"And all of a sudden—you . . . you know that several
of Friedrich's works were still unpublished—a voice
began to make itself heard in the darkness, above the
din of the wheels. Friedrich was singing—enunciating
clearly, though when he talked he used to stutter—he
was singing a poem which was unknown to us; and it
was his latest poem, *Venice*. I don't like Friedrich's
compositions. They're mediocre. But this song . . . well,
by God, it was sublime.

"He had stopped long before we reached the end of
the tunnel. When we came out of the darkness, everything was as it was before. As it was before . . . the same
wretched carriage. The same peasant girl, the hen, the
workmen, and this dentist. And ourselves—and him,

in a daze. That mystery you have just mentioned, I have never since felt it so strongly. All this was so . . . so accidental . . . and Friedrich was much more distressing than a corpse would have been. It was life—I merely say: 'it was life'. Something . . . something very strange was happening: the song was as strong as life itself. I had just discovered something. Something important. In the prison which Pascal describes, men manage to drag out of themselves an answer which, if I may say so, cloaks those who are worthy of it with immortality. And in that carriage . . ."

For the first time he made a fairly sweeping gesture, not with his hand but with his fist, as though he was sponging a blackboard.

"And in that carriage, now, and sometimes since— I merely say: 'sometimes'—the millennia of the starlit sky seemed as completely wiped out by man as our own petty destinies are wiped out by the starlit sky."

He had stopped looking at my father, to whom this unexpected, apparently absent-minded eloquence was all the more disturbing for being of the same kind as his own. Now, he had never seen Walter, even as a child; and this hesitant speech, this impulsive, disordered imagery were not characteristic of Dietrich Berger. But once more Walter had assumed the scornful tone which seemed to be directed beyond my father, at some invisible audience.

"Gratified lovers—'gratified', I believe, is the word?— object to love-unto-death. I've never known it. But I do know that certain works can withstand the intoxication

73

provoked by the contemplation of our dead, of the starlit sky, of history. There are some of them here. No, not those Gothic ones; you . . . know the head of the young man in the Acropolis museum? The first sculpture to have represented the human face, just the human face: free of monsters, of death, of the gods. On that day man also fashioned man from potter's clay. That photograph there, behind you . . . I have had occasion to look at it after looking through a microscope for a long time . . . the mystery of matter doesn't approach it."

From outside came the vast low rustle of the slowly slackening rain on the leaves, like the noise of burnt paper uncurling; the large drop went on expanding, splashing at regular intervals as it fell into a puddle. Walter's voice grew still more restrained:

"The greatest mystery is not that we have been flung at random between the profusion of the earth and the galaxy of the stars, but that in this prison we can fashion images of ourselves sufficiently powerful to deny our nothingness."

Through a skylight somewhere, the mushroom-smell of the trees trickling in the still warm night came in with the rustling sound of the forest silence, mingled with the dusty smell of book-bindings in the library that was submerged in darkness. In my father's head, Nietzsche's singing above the din of the wheels mingled with the old man of Reichbach waiting for death in his shuttered bedroom, the funeral feast, the ridiculous figures that the dead make of those close to them—the metallic thud of the handles of the coffin being carried

74

along on men's backs. This natural gift that Walter was talking about, how much more effective it was against the starlit sky than against sorrow. And perhaps it could have applied to a certain dead man's face, had that face not been a face he loved. For Walter, man was nothing but the "wretched pile of secrets" made to foster these works in the deep shadows surrounding his motionless face; for my father, the whole starlit sky was contained in the attitude of mind which caused a man already possessed by the death-wish to say, at the end of a frequently painful, unglamorous life: "If I had to choose another life, I should choose my own."

Walter drummed nervously with his fingers on the book beneath his hands. My father remembered the face on which the only traces of suicide were a pathetic serenity, the disappearance of wrinkles, the poignant youthfulness of death. And in front of him he saw the almost similar face, the heavy planes of shadow, the staring glassy eyes; and on the table, in the full light, Walter's trembling hands, the same hands as his own, although stronger, the woodcutter's hands of the Bergers of Reichbach, knotted and covered with grey hairs.

2

No SOONER had my father left Walter than he met his cousin Hermann Müller in the corridor. Once famous for his grand love affairs, now fat and bankrupt (a Chartist, into the bargain), this "old gigolo with the natty neck-tie" had been useful to Walter when the latter had been collecting the necessary sum for the purchase of the priory; and he had slipped into the establishment, a general factotum disguised as a curator. He took my father by the arm and led him into a room.

"Walter read us your telegram: 'Most honoured collaborate your research. Best regards'; which didn't sound exactly your style."

My father had wired: "*Arriving Altenburg 2 June*". He appreciated—not quite for the first time—the fortunate time-lag between the reports on his activities and the activities themselves: it was on his return, when he considered himself beaten, that the success he had had a year earlier reached the ears of those he was meeting now. For each of them he had returned, not from a ludicrous, ghostly Afghanistan, but from a Turkey in revolt, from a Tripoli where he had had a price on his head. He found his reputation had preceded him— romantic background, clandestine missions, indifference to gain and maybe to power—as though he had been running close behind it, with long strides that illness had failed to retard; and his hardened features, even more "Hatchet-face" than in Tripoli, fitted it perfectly. He felt, not without embarrassment, like a bankrupt surrounded by spongers.

"I don't think that what I did in Turkey can be of any interest to Walter or to his friends."

"Intellectuals are like women, my dear chap; soldiers make them dreamy: Walter would not have improved on a telegram from Bergson, or from France."

"I'm not a soldier. And I have no intention of taking part in this discussion."

"Oh, so long as you just listen you can't go wrong!"

"It's not that I despise it. Anything to do with European culture is what interests me most these days. What was Walter's connection with Nietzsche?"

"I think his role, not exactly in relation to Nietzsche but in this company, was that of the utter bore who was occasionally useful: rich, with valuable 'friendships', able to pull strings, a pension. . . . He is mean and generous at the same time (and he's not the only one). He is proud of having taken him back to Basle, but in cases like that you could just as well be taken back by your hall-porter. As for the letters he received from Nietzsche, which are the pride of the library and which you, my dear chap, will never read, almost all of them are letters ticking him off."

"That's fine! Has Möllberg arrived?"

"Four days ago. Like you, he arrived late. The great brains have already left, now that the season's over. Daddy Freud was fascinating. By way of compensation, a little psycho-analyst chap was shown the door: at the height of the discussion he suddenly decided he wanted to analyse Walter! Do you know Möllberg?"

After his mission in Mesopotamia, the latter had gone exploring in the territory of the Garamantes. My father had not met him; but on his arrival in Tripoli, having been overtaken by the war in an oasis where he had just started his work, Möllberg had appealed to Enver's adviser, and my father had managed to get him over the

border into Egypt. Hermann pointed to the walls with
a smile:

"This is his room. And they're robbing my poor room
to give my furniture to every Tom, Dick and Harry."

At Altenburg there were countless problems of
precedence, by virtue of age as well as fame: Renaissance
furniture for the internationally famous, Biedermayer
cabinets for the nationally acclaimed, pitchpine cupboards
for the disciples. My father had been surprised at
Hermann's luxurious room. On every bit of furniture
stood strange little figures, some in clay, others in bronze,
which he had at first taken for fetiches: they had been
modelled by Möllberg, who called them his "monsters".
This did not describe them at all. They were imaginary
animals, penguins with cats' faces, squirrels with fins,
fish with ectoplasmic heads, birds of prey with monkeys'
bodies: in a smooth style, as though sculpted in half-
melted fat; and all of them startlingly sad, like Goya's
monsters which seem to remember they were once
human. Some of them, said Hermann, were modelled
over thirty years ago. But all belonged to the same family
of nostalgic gargoyles, and there was something disturbing about this long-standing uniformity of sadness.
Möllberg had given them names: Hargnebouzylle,
Tristophas, Hilaroblique, Malempeine. Some were
benevolent, others malevolent. He used to send them
to his friends.

"You may well smile, my dear chap; but the game has
been going on for over thirty years, and you don't cast
a little monster by the name of Farobolard in bronze

as carelessly as you convert an ink-stain into a beetle, or a problem you can't be bothered to solve into the subject for a discussion.

"Do you know how Walter spends his time? It's wonderful! All the year round you see him bent over his papers: he is drafting The Discussion. It's the contents page of an imaginary book which he isn't writing, and never will write. The result is, he forces others to speak it.

"Another activity of his: bringing what he calls 'their contribution' to bear on his own problem. As long as history was only history, he felt himself secure: man hasn't changed so much, from Tacitus to Momsen or to Michelet."

"Above all, it's action and ambition that haven't changed."

"You're right. What changes more than anything else, my dear fellow, is what people believe in when they don't believe in themselves. Only, long journeys have become an everyday pastime, and ethnology has arrived to upset our historians, who now have to ask themselves if a Roman wasn't as different from them as a Chinaman, for instance. These poor fellows had never gone further than the Barbarians, and they now realise that man has some surprise in store for them. To them the *Weltgeist* is a local phenomenon, but life regarded merely as a Temptation of St. Anthony makes a laughing stock of them. That's why Walter decided to invite ethnologists here.

"Then came his brother's death. It affected him, in

79

spite of their old estrangement. Affected him, perhaps, like a threat. The discussion was to be entitled: 'The Eternal Elements of Art' . . . And now it's: 'The Permanence and Metamorphosis of Man'. Eternity's in a bad way.

"You were surprised he accompanied you on foot: that was to force you to walk at his pace. This discussion is much the same thing.

"The rest of them, of course, play the old elephant trick on him: 'Metamorphosis, art, the bean-sprout? Art and the bean-sprout, Gentlemen, differ from the elephant in that the elephant is an animal of great size and weight, etc. . . .' Discussion on the elephant."

"Then why do men of repute come here?"

"Why should they go elsewhere? They go to hotels: here the company is more intelligent. They go to cafés: here the chairs are more comfortable. The food isn't bad though it's plain, but the neighbourhood is full of charming pubs where the trout-and-almonds is better than you expect, and Rhine wine is worth a thought. At least, that's what they say. Perhaps they're lying also, and they really do come to talk, after all: on the whole intellectuals are chatterboxes. And they end up just the same by talking about what they want to talk about."

Hermann stopped talking, as though caught in the wrong. Möllberg was coming in.

Bald, very tall, very erect, thin as all old men who have lived in the tropics are (when they are not fat), with pointed ears, he looked like a fairy-tale vampire. In brand-new clothes—he had just got back to Europe—his stiff

suit gave him a soldierly look. He had came to con-
gratulate my father, whom he found holding one of his
figurines in each hand.

"You see," he said with a smile, "by dint of making
them, I look like them."

They did indeed look like him, with their Egyptian
beaks hooked like his nose and—almost in every case—
their pointed ears. Above the chimney-piece, near one
of the chief monsters, there was a small hunting-scene
by Cranach, a lovely one.

"I envy Walter," said my father, pointing to the painting.

"No," Möllberg replied. "I brought it with me; just
now I feel the need for German painting."

In this remark my father thought he detected the
nationalistic tendencies for which he was well-known.
He had followed his activities, for every German scientist
dealing with Turkish possessions was sent to the Embassy
in Constantinople. Möllberg had not yet published a
comprehensive work: the lengthy articles which he had
submitted to ethnological journals (and which, through
his discoveries in the realm of pre-history, had turned
African archaeology upside-down) gave a hint of his
ruthless and perfectly coherent interpretation of man. The
prestige which these had given him endowed his decision
to postpone the publication of his book with a significance
which further enhanced the book's importance. On
his return from Egypt into the territory of the Garamantes,
he had crossed the Sahara and, after being forced to go
over certain tracks as many as five times, had reached
German East Africa two years later via the Congo. My

father saw the same methodical insistence in his reasoning; using a clumsy style, with repetitions piled one on top of the other, it looked as if he was bound to create, from the fascinating material he had collected, a synthesis of Hegelian proportions. And it was precisely at a time when the pluralism of civilisations was beginning to come to the notice of a number of intellectuals (and, in particular, my father, who was living in Islam) that Möllberg, obsessed with the idea of order and unity, had begun to exploit a field of study which yielded the greatest number of different theories: ethnology, the idea of man as a strict continuity, a framework for the human adventure.

It was easy to foresee the kind of following his system would attract once it reached the intellectual world with its conflicting schools of thought, for it was the officially recognised German approach to the problems of history; and ever since Hegel Germany in her role of revealer of man's destiny has received violent, impassioned recognition.

"Is the manuscript of *Civilisation, Conquest and Fate* finished at last?" Hermann respectfully enquired.

Möllberg gave him a sardonic look; but his irony was almost aggressive:

"It's burnt."

Taken aback, Hermann had not a word to say.

"When I say 'burnt'," Möllberg went on, "it's . . . synthetic. Its leaves are hanging from the lower branches of various types of tree from the Sahara to Zanzibar. Right. In accordance with tradition, the victorious carry off the spoils of the defeated."

He spread out his arms and added belligerently—
although his belligerence was not aimed at his audience:
"I believe . . ."

He cut short the sentence, shrugged one shoulder:
"It doesn't matter."

And in the same uneasy, sarcastic tone of voice he had
been using:

"Tomorrow we'll see what the rest of them think
about these things."

3

IN SPITE of the summer rain beating on the stained-glass
window, the afternoon light gleamed on the backs of
the books under the mosque-white ceiling. Looking at
the various faces round him, such dissimilar faces,
in many cases bearing the stamp of their country and
yet resembling each other, my father realised to what
degree intellectuals are a race apart. While he listened to
Count Rabaud, the light, shining on the middle of the
main wall which had been submerged in shadow the
evening before, disclosed (where once, perhaps, there
had been a crucifix) a carefully polished figurehead
of Atlas, in the clumsy, pretentious style of nautical
carvings; and above it, two Gothic saints in the same
dark wood.

"Typically Walter," Hermann whispered in his ear,
"in this room he wants nothing but statues in walnut."

Walter, who had only heard the whispering, gave
him a look of disapproval: Count Rabaud was coming to
the end of his talk.

It had taken him thirty years to acquire the airs of a Mallarmé, but he had succeeded. He could be seen every morning, in the corner of the library or under the tall firtrees in the park, declaiming in his fine voice, which he would suddenly lower as if to tell a secret: "Despite the most meticulous research, the most earnest study, we still don't know what Plato really thought about music, or even about beauty."

The Count, whose intense politeness made him submit to Walter's wiles, was linking up the last talks with those still to come, particularly Möllberg's; the deceptively trite argument that he had completed his development was a common one among some intellectuals at that time:

". . . the great artist, gentlemen, demonstrates how the continuity of man is identified with himself. By the manner in which he unfolds such and such an act of Orestes or Oedipus, Prince Hamlet or the brothers Karamazoff, he brings us closer to those destinies which are so far apart from us in space and time; he renders them intimate and revealing. Similarly, certain men have that great gift, that divine quality, of finding in the depths of themselves, and then passing it on to us, the means of releasing ourselves from the bonds of space, time and death."

Walter Berger had begun to pass a vote of thanks (thanks were the order of the day at Altenburg) when Edmé Thirard broke in. He was perhaps the only one of his old friends who appreciated what was admirable in him while treating the rest of him like dirt.

"All the same, my dear Rabaud, there's something

about all this that worries me. Briefly, you admit certain laws of man; you accept the conception of man everlasting, man eternal . . ."

"I believe in eternal man," said the Count with deep, calm conviction, "because I believe in the everlastingness of masterpieces."

("We met in a brothel," Hermann confided to my father. "Do you know what he said in that lovely voice of his? 'We shall never know the truth, my dear Müller, about the extremely strange death of that young lover of George Eliot's.' ")

"Yes," Thirard was saying, "but what have masterpieces ever taught us, what is really meant by 'taught'? My son was about fifteen years old and, rather carelessly, I had just said about something or other: 'That's not how you learn to understand your fellow-men.' To which he replied: 'Oh? Then how?' "

There was silence for a few moments.

The argument which father had been following for the last hour was nothing but a dialogue with culture. An idea was never born of a fact, but always of another idea. Moreover, as far as those round him were concerned, man was the individual, if not the "I"; and for six years my father had had to do too much commanding and convincing to believe that man was not originally other than he is now.

"The question," Thirard went on, "is not one which can be answered in five minutes. All the same, it has the force of innocence behind it; imagine yourselves faced with it."

85

He swept the room with a sardonic glance beneath his bushy eye-brows:

"Come now, I put it to you!"

In a flurry of hands and note-books, a general protest made itself heard above the noise of the rain on the topmost window. All the famous names in the world cropped up, Molière, La Rochefoucauld and Pascal, Hegel and Goethe, Bacon and Shakespeare, Cervantes and others, with the fanatic fervour of people defending something to which they had dedicated their lives. Culture is a religion. But many of them were thinking of the commonplace human mystery as they had come across it in hospitals, in maternity wards, and in the rooms of the dying. As the uproar subsided, a voice could be heard:

"All the same, you can't say that the humanities . . ."

"But yes, that's just it! You certainly can! Culture doesn't teach us about man, it merely teaches us about the cultured man in proportion to his degree of culture; just as self-examination doesn't teach us about man, but merely about the man who is in the habit of examining himself!"

This was not far from what my father had just been thinking.

"I'm not much of a Christian," Thirard went on, "but I do believe that compassion affords us more knowledge—yes, knowledge—about man than all the books I see round me here. Culture, regarded as a be-all and end-all, inevitably results in the production of Chinese mandarins, that's as plain as a pikestaff, my dear friends; the purpose of it has always been to act, if I may say so, as a relative basis for life; but to act as an absolute basis is quite a different thing. As for psychology, well, it teaches one life as much as a battle-scene teaches one how to become a general, or a seascape how to navigate."

"But my dear Thirard," said Count Rabaud, "we still know far more about man than Plato ever knew."

"Christian man, certainly! But the Greek, well, that's not quite so plain as a pikestaff!"

"Once they are analysed, psychic conditions are no longer the same," said Walter. "In ancient times conscience played a small part; our ethical civilisation has made it all-important. But . . . I'm digressing."

His interjections invariably ended with those words. A means of reminding them of the existence of "The Subject" which he had drafted with such care—and vanity, the longing to hear himself answered: "But that's exactly the point."

Thirard kept them to it in a calm, practised, professorial manner:

"Careful now: 'wanting to know', when speaking about man, means two quite different things: on the one hand, investigating causes, preferably a major cause—self-interest, power-complex, anything you like; which obviously leads to a system, to laws. Then on the other hand, a completely different investigation, which takes place in the vast hopfields of the English and Russian novel but which, with us, always leaves a slight taste of sediment, from the full-bodied claret of Montaigne to the dry champagne of Mr. Anatole France."

By no means a drunkard, but mad about the great vintages and little-known local wines which he spoke about as Count Rabaud spoke about George Eliot's young lover, he had given up a first-class appointment at Montpellier University in order to teach at Beaune College.

"Minds devoted to that problem, let's say the Tolstoy of *War and Peace*, Stendhal, Montaigne, Meredith perhaps, Dostoievsky certainly—anyone you care to think of— if they were asked: 'What, in short, do we mean by "knowing about" man?', they would merely reply: 'being incapable of being surprised by him.' That's all. But it's a lot. Not being surprised by him. Negative knowledge? It now seems to be gaining ground on the other investigation, what! It does not result in a system, but in a classification, in a characterology perhaps . . . which is quite natural for, after all, we can hardly ever foresee the really important actions of those nearest to us. We cannot foresee, we cannot know, we can only recognise. It's not for nothing that the word 'exploration', when applied to man, has become a sort of cliché: knowing a country implies having been there! A man we know is a man whose unexpected action can be related almost at once to something already known: the mysterious side to Dupont does not lie in the unforeseen things he does—for then everything would be a mystery—but rather to the impossibility of relating his unforeseen action, when it takes place, to the aspect of Dupont which is familiar to us."

"If I had to have another life," my father could hear

the words, "I would wish for none other than Dietrich Berger's."

"Oh, but just a minute, Thirard, just a minute! There's a factor here which escapes us altogether. Splendid!"

"Stendhal, Tolstoy, careful now! With the great novelists we allow ourselves to be taken in, if I may say so, by sleight-of hand."

Walter coughed. By which he meant: "No bickering." In his indignation the man was bouncing up and down in his chair, which was too small for him (there were never enough chairs at Altenburg); he was a tiny figure with a white beard, hairy and unkempt right up to his cheek bones, and in a frenzy, like a white cat in a ball of wool. His indignation was directed not so much against the sleight-of-hand that had been mentioned as against heaven knows what—the argument, perhaps.

"I once had occasion to visit a friend on his release from prison. A very good friend, a first-class mind. An anarchist-cum-philosopher who had given sanctuary to some downright anarchists following a criminal outrage. An incautious act, but a noble one. A rare quality in a philosopher? Perhaps less so than it seems, after all. But that has nothing to do with it. He had not been allowed to have letters sent to him (there's something in prison regulations . . . but a whole discussion could be devoted to prisons!), but he was allowed to have books. I wanted to ask him what he could have read, I mean, what stood up to prison atmosphere, what kept alive inside there. A splendid question!"

("It must have been the first thing he asked on seeing him again," Hermann whispered in my father's ear.)

"Three books, gentlemen, three books hold their own against prison life."

He cast a bitter, sardonic glance round him:

"*Robinson Crusoe. Don Quixote. The Idiot.*"

"And the Bible," said someone.

"No. That is, I don't know. But there you are: those three books.

"Now, you will observe that they're the same book, one and the same!

"In all three cases" (his speech was becoming less rushed) "we have, in the first place, a man set apart from his fellow men, Crusoe by shipwreck, Don Quixote by madness, and Prince Mishkin by his own nature, by—you see what I'm getting at?—let's say: 'by innocence'. The three isolated heroes of the world-novel! And what are the three stories? The encounter of each of these three with life, the account of his struggle to put an end to his isolation, to get back to his fellow-men. The first struggles through working, the second through dreams, the third through his saintliness. I'm going a bit fast just now, merely a bird's eye view! I know, I know" (he mimicked an imaginary heckler and hastily shrugged his shoulders) "Daniel Defoe wasn't shipwrecked, Cervantes wasn't mad, Dostoievsky wasn't a saint!

"As though humanity lacked desert islands, as though they were not to be found in every corner! Why, our streets are paved with desert islands! And there's always one certain way of being withdrawn from society: through humiliation, shame.

"Now, bear in mind that the three great novels about the reconquest of the world were written, the first by a former slave, Cervantes; the second by a former jailbird, Dostoievsky; the third by a former victim of the pillory, Daniel Defoe."

My father had imagined himself cut off from culture; he now found it almost as familiar as in the days of his first course at Constantinople—contagious.

"Defoe makes use of an exceptional mass of concrete, plastic details, whereas Dostoievsky—'Stendhal and Dostoievsky are the only ones to have taught me anything about psychology,' Nietzsche used to say: taught him what?—uses chiefly the psychological method. But psychological discoveries, psychological distinctions, play exactly the same role with Dostoievsky as plastic distinctions and imagination play in Robinson Crusoe. They are a means of action! Believe in the umbrella and the parrot and you'll end up by believing in Crusoe; believe in the affinity of pride and humility and you'll end up by believing in Rogojin. These psychological discoveries always tend to make us believe in something other than themselves: in the existence of a character and, above all—now here comes the sleight-of-hand!—in the value of a sermon.

"We historians of art, historians of German art in particular, set ourselves face to face with Gothic man or Egyptian man with the lofty intention of eliciting the facts about him! The high-minded desire to know what it's all about! We examine him and we examine ourselves. We draw our discoveries from our characters, if I may say so; but the great artist draws his characters from his discoveries. His psychology is self-examination in the service of a sermon!"

"Well then," said Count Rabaud, "let's apply this self-examination, as we find it in the records of human knowledge, to a Montaigne" (he pronounced it "Montagne") "... to a Rousseau. ..."

"They are not presented to us as we find them! The thing that makes me understand Egyptian man, do I find it in myself? Enough of self-examination! Man begins in a different way."

("Who's that?" my father asked Hermann.

"Don't know. Stieglitz, perhaps.")

Stieglitz was one of the most original commentators on the German Middle Ages: he had published a first-class book, a great part of which was controversial; when he was appointed to Marburg University two years later, he had it republished without re-reading the proofs (it was too long) and sent it, with a gushing inscription, to all the colleagues who were referred to in the script as blockheads.

"Not bad," Hermann went on. "Not bad at all. But all the same, it's the elephant trick again. And then ..."

The man with the beard, like an actor who has just made a wrong exit, pointed a menacing forefinger and added dogmatically:

"Besides, there's no real psychology except in the West." And at last fell silent, decidedly aggressive.

"All the same, it's hard to conceive a great art, a real thought, to which psychology is completely alien!" Thirard exclaimed.

The man with the beard looked at him hesitantly. A murmur indicating approval of Thirard's statement filled the library: the same murmur which, a little earlier, had been raised against him. It voiced the same heartfelt protest as then: everyone felt repelled by a world in which the value of psychology might actually be questioned. The murmur died:

"But what about Islam, to begin with! . . ." said my father.

Walter had repeatedly thrown him an enquiring glance, but got no responses.

A moment during the evening he had spent in Marseilles had just flooded his memory: he was looking into the unlit window of a book-shop. The endless stream of people passing by flowed noiselessly in the depths of the glass. Like the wizards in Eastern fables, the window revealed the thoughts and dreams of all these silent ghosts: Rocambole and Bergson, *The Fire Woman*, a row of Mr. Anatole France's latest novel *The Revolt of the Angels*, Arsène Lupin, thirty classics. In the stream of people flowing mutely past the window, there was Athens and Weimar, the shadows which chased the flickering lights of Balzac's Paris, the pathetic figures in the halo of Dickens' lamps, the crowd of muffled wretches through which, deep in thought, Dostoievsky's murderers plough their way. These classics, whose wealth of human experience and dreams had swarmed

93

through my father's brain as he glanced at their titles, Goethe and Shakespeare and others, Stendhal, Tolstoy, Dickens, these were the *Thousand and One Nights* of the West.

In Eastern fables there were merchants and fabulous birds, princes and jinns: but no man. Islam—the whole of Asia, perhaps—was concerned with God, but with man, never.

"The plastic art of orthodox Islam is abstract," he said, "and its literature imaginative (which is another way of being abstract, of denying man: the jinn and the rosette are inseparable). We've just been told that valid psychology is only to be found in the West; but, in the first place, the *need* for psychology is only to be found in the West. Because the West is opposed to the cosmos, to fatality, instead of conforming to them. And because all psychology is the quest for an inward fatality. The *coup d'état* of Christianity was its establishment of fatality *inside* man—its foundation of it on our nature. The Greek was concerned with his heroes historically—if at all. He gave his demons an external existence in myths, and the Christian gives his myths an internal existence in demons. Original sin is everyone's concern. The crucifixion is everyone's concern."

"Nevertheless, my dear sir," said Count Rabaud shyly, "if the fatality of Orestes depends on the Atrides, the Christian's depends on Adam."

"But because of Adam, or rather Eve, the Christian's fatality has become nature itself. The fatality of the Atrides was only their own."

"And then Christian fatality, individually experienced, is not absolute," said Walter. "Redemption . . ."

"And that's exactly why psychology exists. What does the Christian seek first of all? His salvation. What separates him from it? The fatality of his nature, original sin, the Devil. We have to get to know man in order to understand the ways of the Devil."

"Exactly!" shouted the man with the beard. "And there has been no change. Still the same thing: it's incredible: in psychoanalysis the subconscious, still suspect and *a priori* evil, that's the Devil again!"

Everyone was waiting for my father to go on. In his rather assertive manner they recognised their own vocabulary, their verbal duels and allusions. Intellectuals do not like one of their number being involved in action; but if he makes a success of it they are more curious about him than about anyone else. And my father's activity, more or less clandestine and taking place in the East, was not without its romantic side.

"It's our old struggle against the Devil," he went on, "which makes us confuse our knowledge of man with our knowledge of his secrets. To the question: 'What is man?' we are blindly ready to answer: 'Man is what he conceals.' Which is only acceptable in the West."

"Secrets reveal man to us," said Thirard, "in much the same way as science has disclosed to us the meaning of the Universe."

Walter stirred, as though about to speak, but kept silent.

"Our fiction," my father went on, "—plays and novels

—imply an analysis of man. But it's clear that this analysis by itself would not be an art. In order to become one, it has to be matched with the awareness we have of our destiny."

"Hang it all!" said Thirard distrustfully.

"You don't like that way of putting it? Nor do I."

"Well, I should like to know what you mean by that statement."

"We know that we did not choose to be born, that we would not choose to die. That we did not choose our parents. That we can do nothing about the passage of time. That between each one of us and universal life there is a sort of . . . gulf. When I say that every man is deeply conscious of the existence of fate, I mean he is conscious—and almost always tragically so, at certain moments, at least—of the world's independence of him."

The Hall at Strasbourg . . .

"What is a Greek acanthus? A stylised artichoke. Stylised, that's to say humanised: as man would have made it had he been God. Man knows the world is not on the human scale, and he wishes it were. And when he rebuilds it, it's on that scale that he does so."

Summing up some recent theories, he instinctively assumed the terse style of his conversation and his lectures: discussion always crystallised his thoughts.

"To me our art seems to be a rectification of the world, a means of escaping from man's estate. The chief confusion, I think, is due to our belief—and in the theories we have propounded of Greek tragedy, it's strikingly clear—that representing fatality is the same as submitting to it.

But it's not, it's almost possessing it. The mere fact of being able to represent it, conceive it, release it from real fate, from the merciless human scale, reduces it to the human scale. Fundamentally, our art is a humanisation of the world."

Walter looked at his watch and raised his hand, as though to conduct an orchestra:

"Let us bear this argument in mind: we shall come back to it in the second half of the discussion, as usual. Particularly since, from what our friend Möllberg has told me about the important talk he is going to give, the conclusions he reaches through a completely different intellectual process are not unrelated—I merely say: 'not unrelated'—to the statements you have just heard. And Möllberg will have time to finish before tea."

If little thought was given to food at Altenburg, tea there was sacred.

My uncle's disciples had taken out their note-books; suspense kept the listeners completely still, except for the occasional noiseless movement of a head being tickled by a fly. They knew that the material collected in Africa was of great consequence, and they did not know that Möllberg's manuscript had been destroyed. Sitting bolt upright against the sunny stained-glass window on which drops of water still tumbled and sparkled (it had just stopped raining), with the light shining on his smooth skull and remarkably pointed ears that reminded one of a vampire, Möllberg looked at the same time like some colonel and like his monster Hilaroblique in a brand new suit.

"My dear Mr. Vincent Berger," he said, turning to my father, "I should really like to know what I think about the idea of destiny.

"It leads us at once to the problem which, whether we like it or not, faces all those who are wondering today: 'Is there any meaning to the idea of man?'

"In other words: from beliefs, myths, and above all the multiplicity of mental structures, can one isolate a single permanent factor which is valid throughout the world, valid throughout history, on which to build one's conception of man?"

The evenness of his teeth (false ones, perhaps) was curiously in keeping with the mechanical precision of his speech which was quite different from his heavy, laboured style.

"A century ago we knew only one continent out of the five; today we know every tribe of any importance. Right. Gone are the days when we thought we should understand later—according to the best traditions! Our petition in bankruptcy has been filed.

"It's worrying. It's very worrying.

"The deeper we delve into time, the less we see of primitive, club-wielding cave-man; at the bottom of those dark depths, further down than Ur, than the Sumerian civilisation, than all human archaeology, there are still cities, there is still the state. And since at the back of man—always assuming the word has any meaning —we no longer find the ape, what do we begin to see appearing? A kind of ant.

"Above the governing priesthood was the king. He

rose to power with the moon: invisible at first, he began to show himself when the new moon appeared, and performed minor acts of state. Finally, the full moon made a real king of him, a master of life and death. Then, painted or gilded—looking, perhaps, like a pre-Columbian king—wearing the crown jewels, reclining on a raised couch, he received the sacred lustrations, the blessings of the priests. He administered justice, distributed food to his people, offered up the ceremonial prayer of the kingdom to the stars. Right.

"The moon began to wane: he was confined to the palace. When the moonless period finally arrived, no one had the right to speak to him. Throughout the kingdom mention of his name was forbidden. Suppressed. Daylight was denied him. Hidden away in the dark, even from the queen, he was deprived of his royal privileges. He no longer issued orders. Could neither give nor receive presents. And, of his old status, he retained only this sacred seclusion. Throughout the land, the harvest, marriage, birth were dictated by these events.

"Children born during the moonless period were killed at birth."

He raised a sharp finger, pointed like his ears. The sky had now cleared completely, and the soft light of late afternoon came in through the large window.

"The sexual betrothal of the king and queen—who was always his sister, always—was celebrated on top of a tower; sexual intercourse between the king and his other women was dictated by the movements of the stars. Just as the king's life was dictated by the moon, so the first queen's was by Venus—the planet Venus, of course.

"Now then: when Venus, the evening star, became the morning star all the astrologers were on the look-out. If it coincided with an eclipse of the moon, the king and queen were taken to a mountain cave.

"And were strangled.

"They knew their fate as surely as a uraemia-specialist or cancer-specialist knows the outcome of uraemia and cancer: it was governed by the heavens just as we are by our germs. Nearly all the state officials followed them to their death. They died as a result of the king's death as we die as a result of a blood-clot.

"The king's corpse was tended with extreme devotion until he rose again with the new moon in the form of a new king.

"And everything began all over again.

"That's all."

In this room, filled to the ceiling with books, it seemed that Africa was thinking out loud. Möllberg laid aside his notes, which he had not consulted anyway.

"And all this crops out at the level of history: you know that a representative of the king was solemnly strangled on the main square of Babylon at New Year; meanwhile the real king, the all-powerful, was stripped, humiliated, scourged in some corner of the palace.

"There is no question of this king being likened to a god or to a hero. He was the king in the same way as a queen-termite is the queen. This civilisation lives in complete fatalism. No one in it objects to anything. The king is not sacrificed to a moon-god; he is at the same time himself and the moon, just as the panther-men of the Sudan are at the same time themselves and panthers.

"We are in a cosmic realm, in a realm older than religion, older even than mythology. The idea of the creation of the world has not yet been conceived. One kills in a void. Gods have not yet been born."

By these words my father was reminded of a condition which he too had experienced, the condition in which man is no longer privileged, the pathetic innocence of looking on humanity as one species among others.

"Let's make no mistake about it. I repeat, it's not a question of a religious mental structure: any confusion on that score would make what I have just said meaningless. From the Zend-Avesta to the Koran, man is incapable of being aware of the world except through a religion; in the twelfth century the whole known world thought religiously. Right. But the mental structure implied by cosmic civilisation is as exclusive of that implied by religion as the Christian faith is exclusive of Voltairian rationalism."

Möllberg stopped talking for an instant, and a thousand sounds—voices muttering, chairs creaking—started all at once. The whole room began to breathe.

"Now for another realm," he went on, forthwith commanding a silence broken only by the buzz of flies. "The latest explorations have revealed the existence, in the Melanesian islands, of some extremely instructive native tribes. Their state of civilisation, always assuming the word has any meaning, is not inferior to that which the ethnographer and the missionary normally come across in the Pacific islands. Right.

"Now, these tribes have not discovered the connection between the sexual act and birth—and positively deny it when the missionaries point it out to them: 'The proof that it's false,' they say, 'is that a woman can have sexual intercourse without having a baby.' (The amazing thing, when you come to think of it, is not that this connection has remained a mystery there, but that it hasn't remained one for longer everywhere else.)

"In these tribes the children have no father, in the sexual sense of the word. The one responsible for them, their guardian, is their uncle on the mother's side.

"Think of the number of our social institutions that are based on the knowledge of paternity; imagine what sexual morals would be like without it; think how impossible it was for the missionaries to spread the gospel in a country where 'God has given his Son for man's salvation' and the Incarnation are utterly incomprehensible. These natives feel about the same degree of mystery in the face of birth as we feel in the face of death."

The library was filled with the ringing sound of logs being tipped out of barrows in the nearby square.

"I think I can guess what he's getting at," Hermann whispered (my father could not guess at all).

"We also know," Möllberg went on, "that for certain societies in Australia and Alaska, the exchange system does not exist. They give, and the gift is a sort of challenge from one tribe to the other. Whereas man in our civilisation wants to receive in order to possess, *potlatch* man—

the ritual gift, you know—wants to acquire—through his work, his beasts, his land—in order to give.

"Now remember that exchange is one of the fundamental concepts of all historical civilisations.

"(From the Roman *nexus*, through the Germanic *wadium*, down to the extravagant expenditure of today, there is ample evidence of the *potlatch*, but that's another question.)

"Finally . . . but some of you, perhaps, have been to the Cairo museum. Surely you, Seguin, remember showcase D?

"Examining that case was one of the most important moments of my intellectual life. For a small sum tourists armed with tape-measures can examine and measure its contents. It contains souls.

"The first images of the soul that humanity has ever made."

The tone of his voice altered, as if to indicate he was retracing his steps; it quickly drew attention to an essential point he had forgotten:

"When man stopped being a prisoner in the cosmos, he inevitably encountered death: conceiving an idea of himself meant conceiving himself as mortal. He therefore began to struggle against death. As far back as the earliest days of Egypt the idea of dualism was evolved; but if the corpse decomposes, its double will melt away. Hence the extraordinary business of mummification. However lasting a mummy may be, basalt, of course, is more lasting! So the carved image is added to the mummy. It serves as an emergency body for the double.

"Dualism has often been spoken of as a complex idea. It's quite a clear one: the double is to the corpse what the dreaming mind is to the sleeping body.

"And is, like it, irresponsible.

"Until men invent divine judgment . . . a responsible and rational double, well, that's what is known as a soul.

"The images of the double disappear from the tombs.

"In their place little winged statues appear, which no longer resemble the dead man: the statues in the Cairo showcase. Survival has become immortality. Eternity has replaced time. After a millennium of groping effort, humanity has succeeded in inventing the immortal soul. Right.

"Between the first double and the first soul, the difference of mental structure is, I believe, quite considerable.

"No need to collect a mass of facts. We have just considered societies which are ignorant: the first, of our conception of fate; the second, of our conception of birth; the third, of our conception of exchange; the last, of our conception of death. That's enough.

"Between the men we have just mentioned, and the Greek, or the Gothic man—or anybody else—and ourselves, what is there in common?"

Lowering his lizard-skin eyelids slightly, he paused for a moment, to give more weight to what he was going to say:

"Whether we are talking of God in the religious civilisations, or the link with the cosmos in the preceding civilisations, every mental structure considers as absolute

and unassailable any particular sign which directs life,
and without which man could neither think nor act. (A
sign which does not necessarily guarantee a better life for
man, which can equally well, of course, contribute to his
destruction!) It is to man what the aquarium is to the
fish swimming inside it. It does not enter his mind. It has
nothing to do with the search for truth. It seizes and possesses man, while he never possesses it entirely. So much
so, in fact—and I now come back to Mr. Vincent Berger's
argument—that men are, perhaps, more thoroughly
defined and classified by their form of fatalism than by
anything else."

"Which is ours?" my father asked.

"It's not easy for a fish to see its own aquarium.
. . . First and foremost, one's country, don't you
think?"

Walter raised his hand with the same conductor's
gesture as before and said with a kind of bitterness:

"There is a truth, gentlemen, to which we do in fact
submit, in the same way as those kings who appear on the
fringe, if I may say so, of the most distant past used to
submit to the stars . . . without which neither the idea of
country, nor that of race, nor that of social distinction,
would be what it is. We live in it, as the religious civilisations lived in God. Without it, not one of us—I merely
say: 'not one'—would be able to think. It's our only
realm: it's history."

"And behind history," Möllberg went on, "perhaps
there's something which is to history what history is to
the country, to revolution. Perhaps our consciousness of

time—I don't say 'our concept'—which is of recent date . . ."

"Quite!" (It was the frantic little man with the beard who had spoken about his friend in prison.) "Time, it's miraculous! To have discovered time is the characteristic of modern man! Not only in comparison with Euphrates or Nile man, or with the Greek, but even with mediaeval man! The Middle Ages have no time: when the primitives paint a crucifixion, the figures on Calvary are dressed like the painter's contemporaries! If you want to know exactly what mediaeval time is, imagine a crucifixion with St. John in a bowler-hat and the Virgin Mary under an umbrella. The Middle Ages are an everlasting present. And so, in a different way, is primitive Asia!"

My father once again thought of Marseilles. Whether it was because fashion had, in six years, transformed people's dress, or because of a vague urgency in the tranquil evening, or for any other reason, it seemed that he had not only come back to Europe, but had also re-entered time. Möllberg was going on, stressing his words with his clenched fist for the first time, with a force that was all the more compelling in that everyone could feel the effort he was making to lower his voice:

"It is history's task to give a meaning to the human adventure—as it was the task of the gods. To relate man to the infinite. And the point is to find out whether our civilisation, as it's proclaimed by the best minds in Germany today, carries within itself humanity's past as a man carries within himself the child he once was, or . . . The sky is always the sky, whether it's overcast, or clear, or streaked with cloud; but the only common factor in the three cases is the one to which it does not owe its existence."

He was now speaking with fervour. Outside, men were loading tree-trunks like the ones my grandfather had stacked for forty years in front of the Town Hall at Reichbach, like the ones stacked by the foresters of the Holy Forest in the sun of the Middle Ages—and the fountain in the square was babbling in the evening.

"We are men only through thought; we think only what history allows us to think, and perhaps there's no meaning to it. If the world has any meaning, death should find its place in it, as it did in the Christian world; if humanity's fate is a story with a point, then death is a part of life: but if not, then life is a part of death. Whether it's called history or given some other name, we must have a world that we can understand. Whether we know it or not, that, and that alone, can gratify our yearning for survival. If mental structures disappear forever like the plesiosaurus, if civilisations succeed one another only in order to cast man into the bottomless pit of nothingness, if the human adventure only subsists at the price of a merciless metamorphosis, it's of little consequence that men communicate their ideas and their methods to each other for a few centuries; for man is a chance element, and, fundamentally speaking, the world consists of oblivion."

He shrugged his shoulders and repeated like an echo:
"Oblivion."

Then he thrust his long arms under his neighbour's chair, in quest of his scattered notes.

Discussion and logic, the books in serried ranks on the shelves, were fighting for their rights against the voice of the dark continents. Walter had called on Francis Seguin to speak. The copper-yellow sun gilded the stained-glass window, and the strangled kings and the little souls in rows in the showcase mingled in my father's mind with the people he had rediscovered in Reichbach walking past the spirals of the tall iron doorway, walking past the window of the dead man's room; with that moment when humanity had suddenly seemed so extraordinarily abnormal. In the general amazement caused by Möllberg's talk (they were far from having the German's intellectual grasp of the human adventure!) he vaguely heard Seguin saying that the isolation of civilisations in the course of time, which was probable in face of the millennia, seemed relative, and even doubtful, when speaking about historical civilisations; that he could not feel himself as different from a man of the twelfth century as from an Egyptian of the early dynasties.

"Oh, but just a minute! Just a minute, Mr. Seguin!"

The little man with the beard again:

"We are now losing sight of the argument!" he screeched. "That's very serious! The fate of humanity has a meaning or it has not. Carving the millennia up into centuries does not affect Mr. Möllberg's contention, which is the absurdity or the non-absurdity of the world! God knows I shall make certain reservations on his philosophy, but the position held by the miracle in the mind of Gothic man, think of it! The miracle, eh, the miracle, you realise! Astounding! To think of everything as always subject to a sudden change, a universe in which things have neither weight nor real fatality—only the weight of the unpredictable will of God—where all the past is, in the precise meaning of the word, fantastic! Just try for a minute to think according to the miracle, or even merely by accepting it. All the stress is altered; you feel growing inside yourself a kind of God-knows-what, a metamorphosis. To be convinced that the difference between Gothic man and us lies in the mental structure itself, well, just look at a cathedral! A shell-fish! Polynesian! Tibetan! Come now! To be convinced, you only have to compare a real cathedral with a neo-Gothic church! You only have to look at that!"

With both his hands and his beard, he pointed to the two Gothic statues, the good thief and the bad, standing on either side of the Atlas.

Greek marbles have an inward look, my father thought, but good Gothic ones always look like blind men trying to see. . . like these men round him, at the mercy of the devil of an intelligible world.

"The miracle, all right, all right! But even so," Thirard was saying, "in the twelfth century men lived as members of society, they traded, etc. We are no longer talking of pre-history. When I listen to you, Stieglitz," (So the man with the beard was Stieglitz!) "it seems to me that Gothic man is the author of Gothic art, in the same way that Rubens is the author of the pictures by Rubens; all the same, he did something else as well! Where does my friend Dupont come into all this? When I want to know exactly what I think, I call for Dupont!

That the psychic realm of an Egyptian high priest is in no way that of a cardinal—nor, *a fortiori*, that of a business man or a professor like myself, I am perfectly prepared to believe; but the difference that Möllberg here considers as fundamental, can he see it between the Egyptian workman and the workman from, say, Alsace?"

This was what my father would have asked had he not preferred to keep silent. "Man is what he achieves," he had told Walter.

"Christianity," Möllberg replied, "is full of people who are not Christians. I'm not referring to those who are atheists, of course. No, the ones I have in mind are nothing; quite simply, they are nothing. And that has always been so, except in so far as numbers are concerned. Even in the Middle Ages. Was Egypt full of workmen who were not Egyptians? Maybe. Right. What does that matter? Man is not interesting in himself, he is so by reason of what really makes him man; it is in that, unfortunately, that his fundamental difference consists. The more men partake of their civilisation, the more they resemble one another. I agree! But the less they partake of it, the more they fade away. The everlastingness of man can be conceived, but it's an everlastingness in nothingness."

"Or a fundamental one?"

It was my father who put the question. The point at issue was no longer the history of man, but the nature of every individual; and everyone felt himself at stake. Möllberg smiled, in the same sour way as when he had told Hermann his manuscript had been destroyed.

"Fundamental man is a myth, an intellectual's dream about peasants: just try to dream about the fundamental workman! Will you have it that for the peasant the world is not made of oblivion? Those who have learnt nothing have nothing to forget. A wise peasant, I know what that is; but it's not fundamental man! There's no such thing as fundamental man, developed, according to the age he lives in, by what he thinks and believes: there is man who thinks and believes, or nothing. A civilisation is not an ornament, but a structure. Look! We all know our friend Walter's craze: those two Gothic sculptures and that figurehead are of the same wood, as you know. But those forms are not shaped from fundamental walnut, but from logs of wood."

"But even so," Thirard replied, "logs, my dear Mr. Möllberg, after all! Logs, that's a metaphor . . . a mere metaphor."

"A mask. The truth is: the animal.

"Outside thought, we have sometimes a dog, or a tiger, a lion if you insist: anyhow an animal. All men eat, drink, sleep and fornicate, of course: but they do not eat the same things, do not drink the same things, do not have the same dreams. The only thing they have in common is sleeping, when they sleep without dreaming—and being dead.

"Whether nothingness is everlasting or not, what does it matter to us, if the very thing that gives man his dignity is forever condemned! If the tenacity of the best only achieves what is most perishable . . ."

"That tenacity, at least, is lasting, my dear Möllberg," said Count Rabaud. "Something eternal lives in man— in thinking man—something that I shall call his divine quality: it's his ability to call the world in question."

"Sisyphus too was eternal."

Stieglitz rose to his feet:

"But just a minute! Just a minute, now! The great line of Hegelianism remains intact. The point at issue is the integration in the *Weltgeist* of the facts acquired through our new knowledge, and I can't for the life of me see why what you call the human adventure should not become a history, just as the history of Germany is a history, although consisting of elements which at first glance seem heterogeneous. I would even say that we Germans, released from the prejudices of classicism, are particularly qualified to bring such a history to its successful conclusion!"

"That's what I've been saying for years!" Möllberg replied with the suppressed fury of an incurable to whom one has incautiously mentioned his disease. "It's a good thing to be released from the classical prejudices, but we must not at the same time be released from the bonds of truth!

"Humanity's successive psychic states are invariably different, because they do not affect, do not exploit, do not involve the same *quality* of man. Fundamentally speaking, Plato and St. Paul can neither agree with each other nor convince each other: they can only convert each other. A Christian king and a pre-historic king whose life is dictated by the stars have not got two *ideas* of destiny: for the Christian king to be aware of destiny, for him to conceive it, the other king's psychic world must first disappear. I doubt if there's any communication between the caterpillar and the butterfly. Even between the Hindu who believes in the absolute and the transmigration of souls, and the Westerner who believes in the fatherland and in death, any communication is artificial. Is love of painting a particular means of understanding music? The communication begins when India and Europe condense their psychic states into ideas. But what is the idea of a state, of a feeling, if it isn't the memory of it?"

"Yes, but even so! Just a minute! I should not like . . . but, after all, you . . . Your work is the result of ten years' toil, Mr. Möllberg, and . . ."

"Fifteen years!"

" . . . and you don't abandon such conclusions out of sheer wantonness! A final, overwhelming concept must have obtruded itself! You, more than anyone else, have proclaimed Germany's intellectual mission!"

"If the human adventure had any meaning, then Germany would be chosen to give it expression."

"My God, I can't believe it! But what concept could have made you abandon . . ."

"It wasn't a concept! It was Africa."

The endless succession of days under the dusty firmament of Libya or the heavy leaden sky of the Congo, the tracks of invisible animals converging on the water points, the exodus of starving dogs under the empty sky, the time of day when every thought becomes a blank, the giant trees gloomily soaring up in the prehistoric void . . .

"I'm the most qualified commentator on Africa in the world," Möllberg went on with sardonic self-satisfaction;

113

"there's no better way of concentrating on man than looking at ant-hills."

Walter, who had been a little worried to see the discussion taking this turn, began to sum up the talk, which was
the usual procedure when a talk was finished. Before
speaking, Möllberg had given him some notes. My father
thought of the leaves hanging from the trees . . .

"Is there any factor," Walter was reading, "on which
we can base the notion of man . . ."

The discussion over, everyone was free until dinner
time. My father went off across the fields.

They lay behind the priory between two patches of
wood, speckled with the stars of wild chicory the same
blue as the evening sky—a sky now as clear as the sky at
high altitudes—in which fleeting clouds were drifting.
Everything growing out of the earth was cradled in a soft
radiance, bathed in the dust of the gathering twilight;
leaves still shone with a polished brilliance in an atmosphere quivering with the last cool breezes born of the
grass and the brambles. At Kabul, at Konya, my father
was thinking, the only talk would have been about God.
. . . How many odd problems had been investigated
with the same fervour under the very vaults of this
priory! The sun was setting, kindling the red apples on
the apple-trees. Idle thoughts, orchards eternally re-born,
which the same fears always kindle like this evening's
sun. Thoughts of long ago, thoughts of Asia, thoughts
of this rainy, sunny summer day, so accidental, so rare—
like the white race of men in the Marseilles evening, like

for a man of thought. In civilian life, he had at least been able to choose some of his superiors. What he liked about war was the masculine comradeship, the irrevocable commitments that courage imposes; but he hated the Imperial Army (although he was certain he would not have liked any other army any better).

Immediately after the first victories in the east, after the nights when the whole front was ablaze with Russian rifle-butts smashed up and used as fuel for the army, he had applied for a transfer to the Military Mission in Turkey. Whether it was because the German Army appreciated civilian qualifications about as much as any other army, or because Liman von Sanders' staff did not care to see a man in Constantinople who was regarded by many as a personal friend of Enver's and whose patriotism was not his outstanding quality, or whether—on the contrary—it was because the Secret Service had earmarked my father for other schemes, he had been assigned on a long-term posting to the Co-ordination of Reports (in his view, the most important section of a modern secret service). Then he had been put at Captain Wurtz's disposal.

Three days after his arrival, the Captain had ordered him to take down the interrogation of a female prisoner whom Wurtz suspected of being La Rosnowa, one of the best Russian informers. Her passport, a false one no doubt, was in order, but Wurtz had discovered that La Rosnowa's child happened to be at school in Lodz when the town was taken, and had sent for him.

After ordering the woman to be brought in, he asked all his colleagues—except my father—to leave the room. She must have been in the corridor already, and at the sight of these Secret Service officers walking past her, one after the other, to leave her alone with their chief, she probably feared the worst. When her guard finally shoved her into the office, she stopped for a second in front of the door, which had closed behind her, then suddenly moved towards Wurtz, going on with a sentence she had started:

". . . that I'm having to undergo is absolutely unbelievable!"

And reaching the desk, in a still louder voice, as though on the point of a nervous breakdown:

"For heaven's sake! It's absolutely illegal . . ."

"That's quite enough!" Wurtz shouted.

In the tone in which he would have shouted: "Halt!" to a company. And at once he resumed his normal voice, pointing to a chair:

"Please sit down, madam."

She still hesitated, as though she had not heard or had not understood. As she remained silent, my father, having nothing to take down, was able to observe her closely. They had stripped her in order to search her and had given her a black smock, like a schoolgirl's pinafore. Her face was a perfect oval, the strange, striking, Easter-egg oval of certain Russian women. She might perhaps have been beautiful had it not been for the night in the cells. She sat down, keeping her eyes on Wurtz, more bewildered by his sudden politeness than by

his brutality. She rubbed the palms of her hands on the
black smock, as if she wanted to wipe them dry forever.

"Your identity, please."

She recited her passport particulars.

"Married?"

"No, sorry," she said with a smile.

"So am I," Wurtz replied. "So, no children?"

"For heaven's sake!"

There was something theatrical about her "for heaven's
sake!" that made her Russian accent still more pronounced.
Indeed, everyone in this office with its flaking Central
European walls was playing a part. Wurtz made a
movement with his hand, as though to apologise.

"But I should like to know," she went on, "what
is there against me?"

Wurtz had in front of him a copy of the interrogation
she had been through immediately after her arrest.

"We're going to try and clear this up," he said.
"First of all, what were you doing in Prczyba?"

She embarked on a cover-story as perfect as every
story prepared "in the event of things taking a nasty
turn". To each of her statements the Captain nodded
his head, as though in agreement. And the woman felt
her seductive powers coming back, exploited them,
tried to create between Wurtz and herself an atmosphere
of intimacy over and above the wretched demands of
war: besides, she realised her obligations, but even so . . .
She looked at him with anxious intensity: he was a
giant of a man with a snub nose and small glinting eyes,
a fairly pleasant Pinocchio puppet face. Still rubbing

her hands on her black smock, like a cook in the presence of her employer, she suddenly became aware of her clothes, of the frightful state of her hair, and her tone of voice and expression altered as though she had been slapped. But her sex was now her only weapon, and she at once began to exploit it again with all her might. Wurtz nodded his agreement more and more.

"A person who operates as cleverly as you," he said at last, "obviously realises that at this moment she's heading straight for the firing-squad."

"You don't shoot women!"

She looked him straight in the eye, and for the first time appeared intent not on winning him over, but on standing up against him.

"You seem very sure of that! You have thought about it—more than is necessary, perhaps, for the lady of your passport."

He took a paper out of a file and began reading aloud the account of the execution of a woman who had been shot a fortnight before.

At the fourth line she had understood. The Captain went on reading and occasionally glanced at the woman's hands: like my father, he had noticed her strange habit of wiping them. She now held them still in her lap. When he had finished:

"But for heaven's sake," she asked, shrugging her shoulders slightly and opening her eyes wide, "what's that got to do with me?"

"It has got something to do with you," Wurtz gravely replied.

Smiling again, she began to explain where and how her passport had been issued by the German occupation authorities. While she was speaking, facing Wurtz and my father, the door silently opened; the woman had her back to it. Against the dark, dismal background of the corridor a boy could be seen approaching, with some of Wurtz's agents behind him. A boy of about twelve, like any other boy: fair-haired, with a tumbling forelock and small prominent ears. Feeling nervous, he stopped. He was wearing a cape and carrying a school cap in his hand. My father could see simultaneously the woman who still kept smiling and the child in the background behind her. Why the devil had he always imagined that spies never had any children? He felt he would not be able to take down the interrogation.

At least the child had not recognised her voice. He was looking at a Russian aeroplane bomb which was lying on the desk.

"Your organisation makes excellent passports," said Wurtz. "So does ours. But yours has . . . we'll see about that later."

"Has what?"

The guard gave the child a slight push so that he moved forward again; the boy dropped his cap. The woman heard the cardboard peak strike the tiled floor behind her and, as though this noise had been heard not by the person she was trying to be, but by the terrified person she was concealing, she suddenly looked round, overturning her chair.

Amazed to discover behind her a child almost on all fours (he was picking up his cap) when she was expecting a threatening blow, she at once looked round at us again, then again behind her. My father now had only a back view of her, but he could see the child full-face, who was now on his feet again looking at her, gaping: he had not yet recognised her. As though to draw away from him, she was pushing the table with all her strength on to my father's knees, which were wedged against it. The child absent-mindedly put his cap back on his head, took it off again at once. His glance, which had shyly strayed over the desk, shifted back to the woman, whose arms, from her shoulders right down to her hands that clutched the desk, were quivering like ropes.

Perhaps the child had never seen her like this, with her hair undone, and in a black smock. "Don't recognise her!" my father was thinking, as though his thought could have any effect. She must have drawn away from him for the sake of caution, and perhaps Wurtz's information was wrong. But how could he fail to see the convulsive movements of her arms?

With a gentle push from the guard, the child took two steps forward. A smile, slight at first, then more pronounced, lit up his little face. He went up to the woman whose arms were now no longer trembling.

"Don't be frightened," said Wurtz in a fatherly manner, "do as you like, do as you like."

The child looked at his kindly, boot-button eyes, scared and attracted by them at the same time. My father did not realise it was possible for him to suffer so much shame. His muscles contracted, as they do when waiting for the burst of a shell.

Approaching the woman who still did not move, the child turned to the left, and came up and stroked the bomb.

What does it matter what followed? The child was not the woman's child. But what my father was never to forget was that small, smiling face picked out to act as a perfect instrument of treachery. "Methods like these, which you shrink from," the Captain had said, "save the lives of thousands of our soldiers. In Turkey, did you work with goody-goodies?" For the first time he showed he knew more about my father than just his name. My father was thinking that commanders should not have to do their own dirty work: his role had been that of a political, not a police, agent. Besides, Wurtz's self-satisfaction over the trick had not escaped him, and he was afraid that the trick would have been employed far less skilfully by anyone who did not enjoy this self-satisfaction. ("You're a pretty good swine," the woman had told Wurtz as soon as she saw through it, even though her teeth were chattering; to which he had replied: "You'll look pretty, too, when you're shot.") My father had no wish to argue. He asked permission to leave the Secret Service, and nothing was done to keep him. Perhaps this assignment of his had been in the nature of a test.

So he was now waiting for another posting. How could it be that he was ordered to report today with Captain Wurtz? As soon as the latter arrived, he asked him.

"I don't know. Yesterday the Chief of Staff asked for the records of press officers with university degrees. And then we need more and more clever officers for Intelligence Co-ordination."

The orderly came to fetch them.

Was the General thinking about the flies, the weak points in his division or the consequences of what he was about to tell them? He did not look at them, he looked out of the window.

"Gentlemen, an attempt at . . . chemical warfare, a gas attack, will take place tomorrow."

An attempt had been made a month before. The wind had changed, or something had gone wrong; the attack had not taken place. Did the gas work chemically, or by means of bacilli, or simply by restricting the air supply of whoever it encircled? The sound of crickets could be heard. It was to them that the General seemed to be speaking, and to the fields smiling in the sun.

"Professor Hoffman, he's one of the inventors of this . . . method of warfare, will be arriving from Lodz this evening by car between seven and eight o'clock. You'll find him at Colonel von Lüdow's command post. You'll be given the target area there. You won't have to worry about the experiment, or the preparations for it. The Professor will follow it from as close a position as possible. Your only orders are to bring him back safe and sound."

And still talking to the crickets:

"Nothing untoward must happen to him, at any cost, whatever the circumstances."

My father had never heard an order given in such an offhand manner. Yet it was an order. Was the General wishing he was elsewhere, was he simply thinking about something else? His gaze wandered back into the room, rested for a moment on the two bewildered officers.

"You can make the necessary arrangements."

As the car stopped, Captain Wurtz and my father saw their salute acknowledged by the sweeping movement of a broad-brimmed felt hat; a hand threw back a scarf worn like a muffler (in June), another threw a half-smoked cigarette at their feet: hands, cigarette, muffler, longish grey hair, a whole dovecote seemed to fly out of the Professor's face. A clean-shaven face, which was rare at that time, all hooked and angular, like certain Aryan faces that look like Jewish faces only sharper. A big quiet fellow followed him out of the car, a lovely suitcase in his left hand, an improbable-looking basket in the other: his son.

"Pleased to meet you," said the Professor amiably, pulling a mournful face. "I'm really extremely pleased. I've always had a special regard for Intelligence Officers."

He put his arm through Wurtz's, who stood dumb-founded, with his heels still together.

The *Europa* was the least shabby of the three requisitioned hotels in Bolgako. One of its garden walls having been destroyed by a shell (the town had been bombarded by Germans and Russians in turn), everyone had made a habit of going in through the gap, over the flower beds. Across the sky which was as clear as ever, and serene now that night was falling, in the perfume of dusty roses which had not yet withered, the thunder of guns reverberated from the ground in the solitude of this vicarage garden.

The table was laid in the Captain's room. His batman had found some of those long, thin Polish sausages which are eaten raw. With a sorrowful air the Professor put his hat down at the foot of the chimneypiece, drew a flask and a yellow bottle out of his basket, and took a gulp from the neck of the bottle.

"For my asthma, gentlemen! But this—" (he held up the other flask) "this, mind you, is genuine French brandy."

Sadly he put it on the table.

"Until the day we go to France and get it for ourselves. Let's eat: tomorrow morning the Russians are going to cave in."

Still distraught.

Before coming to the Captain and my father, he had inspected the containers and the gas-launching apparatus.

"Don't the preparations come up to your expectations, Professor?" Wurtz asked.

"They're perfect," he answered with the utmost dejection.

My father went down to fetch the beer. When he came back, with the mugs fanning out round his fists, the Professor, with hair all over the place, his son and the Captain were bent over some photographs: the first one, lying between the plates, was of the house where the Professor had always lived. It was going to be pulled down to make room for an airfield. He had hoped to save it; one of the telegrams he found waiting for him here had brought a definite refusal. Hence his concern. The other photograph was of Wurtz's two children. Yet the Captain was not exactly sentimental; but in the Professor my father sensed the infectious power of those extreme neurotics who impose the atmosphere of their own genius or madness. There was something "shaman" about this man, but it was a disturbing shamanism.

While Wurtz was putting the photograph back in his pocket, as though trying to hide it, the son was rummaging in his wallet. He also took out a photograph, which he held as a gambler holds a winning card before throwing it down on the table.

"It's my turn, I'll show you my children."

What was the meaning of this sentimentality? Wurtz had just bent in amazement over the photograph which had now been put down next to the one of the house. My father looked at it: three bulldogs.

"Max was an undergraduate at Oxford," said the Professor. "He specialised in animal medicine. By vocation, mind you!"

"By inclination," said big Max in a dreamy voice. And with a slight bow, as though he was being introduced, he added in a tone of self-satisfied modesty: "A veterinary surgeon."

The odd part about it was that the dogs looked like him. There was something wildly improbable about this conversation in the low-roofed room, with the distant gunfire and the wonderful evening light in the only window. Although Bolgako was in Austrian Poland, the room was Russian: the soft evening light conjured up a picture of the rough texture of old walls under their recent coating of lime, a world of lizards, dry-rot and mouse-holes. The Professor would be fighting the bed-bugs all night long.

The Captain was pursuing his own train of thought:

"Are we merely going to do a test tomorrow, Professor —don't tell me, of course, if you don't think you ought to—or is it to be a real attack? It depends on which it is, what measures we take for your personal safety. And as the last attempt failed. . . ."

"The tests that have been made up to now on this front, really!"

He burst into childish laughter: like the great apes, he was alternately senile and infantile, but never young.

"They tried to use poison. But that's utterly mad! Hydrocyanic acid and carbon monoxide are perfect poisons, what result did they have? You need half a gramme of hydrocyanic acid to a cubic metre of air: the victim is seized with convulsions and falls dead in a tetanic rigor. It's perfect. In an enclosed space. But so what? The target area, you realise, happens to be in the open air!"

He got up and managed to walk up and down in the room by stepping sideways between his son's chair and the stove.

"Then what? They tried carbon monoxide. In a laboratory. A formidable toxic agent, with all the requisite qualities, easy to prepare, cheap. It solidifies the haemoglobin in the blood, prevents it from mixing with the oxygen in the air. But there's still the problem of the open air!

"I've discarded poisons. We shall be using . . . something else. We've gone further than the chlorine derivatives. It looks elementary, chlorine does, but it's not so dusty, you know! Easy to liquefy, disastrous to the human organism, very cheap, mind you! According to your . . . colleagues on the Western front, gentlemen, our chemical attack on the Yser last month caused between ten and twenty thousand immediate casualties: it was more than was needed to make the English line cave in! But, unfortunately, it can be seen!"

Still pacing up and down, he sighed under his grey locks:

"The enemy will use masks, and we'll have to begin all over again."

"When you discard poisons," my father asked, "what do you have to aim at, then? The respiratory organs?"

The Professor spread his arms wide in a ballet-dancer's gesture. "But the mucous membranes, my dear sir! It's quite simple: the mucous membranes!

"We've got some compounds which are more effective than chlorine," he said, taking a drink. "Naturally! Phosgene is ten times as strong as chlorine, but phosgene . . ."

He was passing the window: he opened it wide, put his hand out to test the wind. On the other side of the garden the onion domes and the cross of an Orthodox church shone in the evening light at the end of the sloping main square. My father felt himself hemmed in by Russia, not so much because of the gold and purple cupolas, but because of the old pavements of the bulging square, uneven as shingle and illuminated, it seemed, at ground level by the last beams of the setting sun; beyond the rose-coloured streets, the invincible Russian past was the only thing alive in the evening and the breathless silence of the war. The Professor's voice was summing up the advantages and disadvantages of phosgene, and my father was conscious of the depth of the Slav world extending as far as the Pacific. In the trees there were still a few birds; others were returning to their nests, with the hoarse, anxious cheep of the swallows carried from afar as darkness fell. The Professor threw his extinguished cigarette out of the window, which he shut, and came back beaming with joy:

"The wind's still perfect, still perfect! Anyway I'm less frightened of a change of wind than of a sudden dampness."

He had already lit another cigarette and started pacing up and down again.

"But we're still at the level of pre-history in chemical warfare! Ethyldichloride sulphate is perhaps the best fighting gas of all. A caustic product, blistering and poisonous at the same time! Particularly dangerous, mind you, since the victim is not affected at the actual moment of poisoning: it begins to take effect several hours afterwards . . ."

He stopped talking; his hand was still moving, the sausage in it beating time to humanity's funeral march.

"And even then . . ."

He kept them in a state of suspense that seemed to give him physical pleasure, then suddenly appeared to forget them.

"Eight centigrammes vaporised . . . a cubic metre of
air," he murmured, "fatal casualties in under half an
hour. Effective—it's marvellous—up to . . . up to . . ."

He could not get through his mental calculation.
He took out a fountain pen, looked for something on
the table; Max snatched up the photograph of the dogs;
his father seized the one of his beloved house and turned
it over, then began to scribble down some figures.
It was difficult to see. The Captain lit a paraffin-lamp.
The Professor went on with the calculations he had
started on the back of the snapshot and got up. He looked
at the officers as though they were the enemy—eyes half-
shut, jaw slightly tilted:

"Effective up to one part in fourteen million parts of air."

And waving his photograph like a proof:

"Perhaps chemistry is the final weapon, the superior
weapon, which will give the people who use it properly
—who master it!—world-wide supremacy. Perhaps even
the Empire of the World!"

The lamp-light had suddenly made the window black
and opaque. Beyond it, my father was still conscious of
Russia and its sunflowers blooming in the night as far
as Mongolia.

"Isn't it likely that the enemy Intelligence Service
could soon get hold of our formulae?" asked the Captain.

"But in less than six months we shall have used six
different kinds of gas! You see, between the production
of the various kinds of gas and the means of protection
against them, the same race will go on as was started
thousands of years ago, since . . . the first manufacturer

133

of the bludgeon, between the lance and the breastplate, the bullet and armour-plating. Only, and this is the most important side of the question . . ."

He started pacing up and down again, creating the same suspense he had created once already:

". . . all the time that struggle has been going on, it's never been armour-plating that has scored the winning run."

There was a short silence.

"Professor, you did say, didn't you," asked Wurtz, "that the latest discoveries are capable of poisoning the enemy troops without their knowing it?"

"Sufficiently so for the fighting spirit of the evacuated troops to be reduced to zero against a fresh attack."

Wurtz smiled uneasily, like an overgrown child caught in the wrong. The Professor lit another cigarette, stopped pacing up and down, and said nothing. He knew what the Captain was thinking. He waited. Wurtz shook his head, looking resigned but not in agreement.

"In this war that's being waged against us by the whole world," the Professor said at last, almost gently, "Germany has no choice.

"Victory will save the lives of hundreds of thousands of our soldiers. And the most effective ways of achieving it are the best ones."

Once again he brandished the photograph of his house:

"One part in fourteen million of air!"

And armour-plating is always less strong than a shell, my father reflected.

"I admit that," said the Captain. "But . . . can you tell me why we are despised?"

He began to trace stars on the table-cloth with the point of his knife.

"If you look at it objectively," said the Professor in a voice of authority, "gas constitutes the most humane method of warfare. For gas, mind you, announces its presence! The opaque cornea first goes blue, the breath starts to come in hisses, the pupil—it's really very odd! —becomes almost black. In a word, the enemy is fore-warned. Now, if I think I still have a chance, even a faint chance, I'm brave; but if I know in my heart of hearts that I haven't, then courage is no use. Nothing to be done about it!"

To the Captain, these two men were enemies. Men of words and figures, "intellectuals", who wanted to do away with courage. They were belittling it. His own courage was real enough: when taken prisoner by the Russians and condemned to death, he had refused to give the least bit of information, although he was promised a hundred thousand roubles and his freedom in Russia— and had escaped. This fortitude, in his eyes, justified everything, gave him every right. He shook his round, snub-nosed head, as though bothered by invisible flies.

"It'll be a great misfortune," he said, "if we're to see the old German method of war vanish from the Empire."

My father was listening, watching Wurtz turning into a moralist (not to mention the other moralist). In the same way as one watches a madman who looks a bit like oneself. Contrary to my father's views, the Captain had justified the introduction of the child in the name of the soldiers he was saving; and the Professor was repeating the same argument. Well, well, this room was full of saints!

"Yes," said the Professor drily, "but Germans are also men, and subject to weaknesses, what?"

He took three steps towards the window:

"Sulphate, that's incorruptible."

And began spinning round his forefinger a key he had suddenly taken from his pocket. Once more he leaned towards the darkness, then turned round:

"Look," (all of a sudden his voice was louder) "you're sure your people won't make a hash of the containers?"

"Your instructions will be followed to the letter."

With a nod of approval he started his ant's crawl again. My father went to the window; the wind had not changed. The guns could no longer he heard; shovel-strokes sounded in the distance, above the slow, sad footsteps of a horse. All the stars were out, thick as nebulae. Some cavalry were gliding past in the depths of the night, dispelling the sadness forced into the heart by the monotonous presence of the encircling worlds: there was too much war on the face of the earth for metaphysical fears. In the room they went on talking . . . Only a moment in the "struggle between the lance and the breastplate, ever since the first manufacturer of the catapult". And my father looked up at the night sky, as though he had suddenly been made a miraculous, personal gift of the millions of nebulae.

"You see, it's just as I said!"

Over my father's shoulder the Professor had stretched his hand outside.

"Conditions are still perfect . . . perfect!"

The horse's footsteps dwindled till they mingled with the clatter of the squadrons moving up to the front. The garden, the gap in the wall and the tea-roses were lost in the darkness; the golden crosses of the cupolas were now black against the birdless sky. The cool night breeze was blowing loyally in the direction of Russia.

2

AT FIVE in the morning, my father, the Professor and Wurtz arrived at the front line. The gas containers were in position, in the places the Professor had picked out the evening before. Lying parallel in the trenches, they looked like bottles of compressed air; in ranks like soldiers they seemed, despite the men at their posts behind them, to have taken the place in battle of the German army.

The men came back to the dug-out which they had been allotted. They were to move forward when the gas-launching started; the Professor having declared that the time of the attack was immaterial, the decision had been left to the command.

The troops were drawn up in the trenches. My father and his two companions went through a huge cavern streaked with light, a bar of sunlight lodged in every observation-hole. The eyes of the company dug in there —the 132nd—had not yet got used to the semi-darkness and could only make out the nervous gestures of battle-tension. A smaller dug-out communicated with the first. They took up their positions there. As they were going up to one of the three observation-posts, my father could hear the Professor, who had remained behind, addressing the uniformed shadows:

"Everything all right, you fellows? Everything all right, what?"

Which was barely answered by the growl reserved for civilians. The son was probably skipping along behind. Glued to his observation-hole, my father did not turn round.

Beyond the tall tufts of grass which trembled from the deep vibrations of the gunfire, the shells up-rooted two lines of trees at random, behind and in front of the Russian trenches. The Germans were holding one side of the valley, the Russians the other, further down; between them, still untouched by the morning sun and hidden in a misty shadow, the river flowed towards Szapewo which stood between the two slopes, at the bottom of the vast triangle of sky. Although the sun had outlined the wooden houses on top of the high ramparts for the last hour, the bombardment of the town had not yet started. Only the trees on the dark fringe of the wood kept bouncing into the air in the death leaps of bowled-over rabbits. The grass tufts quivered with the gunfire, and behind the Professor, whose felt hat shook against the spike of my father's helmet, the latter could feel the suspense of the company on watch.

"And you have absolutely no idea of the time of the attack?" the Professor asked for the tenth time. "No means of cross-checking? No method of deduction?"

They had now been waiting for three hours. He was pacing up and down in the shelter as he had done yesterday in the room, his nose sticking out, engulfed in his muffler. The son was dreaming—about his dogs, perhaps? The soldiers' nervous suspense had subsided without disappearing, like an acute illness that had become a chronic one; during the last year each one had got used to the fact that his own fate did not depend on himself. My father could hear groups of them talking together. To pass the time, Wurtz had told him what he knew about the men who were talking. In the rectangle of the observation-hole it seemed as if beyond the river, which was now filled with brilliant sunshine, the enemy would remain inactive for all eternity; behind my father, odd words mingled with the noise of the weapons, violent arguments started up and died down and were finally drowned in the ceaseless thunder of the guns.

"The Czar!" said one voice. "Wipe out Germany!" (A paper was being unfolded). "Wipe out Germany! He stays behind in his palace, at Petersburg! Underground! A pretty sight! And the people who are pricks enough to listen to him! Frederick the Great, I've never thought much of that chap: because I say it's cheek to go and seize someone else's country. Yes, cheek! But there's something to be said for him, you fellows; he at least led his army himself, and he marched at the head of his men!"

"Frederick! In those days they used to fight with spears and slings!"

"The French have more, they've got rifles," said a third voice, chipping in.

139

"Under Frederick the Great? Silly sod!"

"You're the sort of chap, when they wake you up at night to stand you a mug of beer, you think it's a snap check, and then you talk about Frederick the Great! It makes me sick!"

"Frederick drew up the plans, and he also marched in front! In front! You can say what you like about him, but when it comes to the army he was champion, I'm telling you! While that other prick, the Czar, he sticks in his fortress! In his underground fortress! And even then he wears a suit of armour!"

"Armour!" said the other voice scornfully.

"Armour, I'm telling you! You're not going to try and tell me you know anything about it, a chap like you who's never been out of Bavaria. I'm telling you, he wears a suit of armour!"

"Look, you know what? You make me sick! Armour!"

"Christ, Ludwig, I'm telling you, he wears armour!"

This indignant protest was drowned in a general uproar in which the only words to be heard were:

"That won't be much good to him against gas...."

The argument shot off like a ferret into another dark corner and was succeeded by another conversation, this time a private one:

"It's not all manual labour in my job, it's more brain-work."

"You a fitter?"

"Metal-cutter."

"Yes, that's like me, in die-stamping, it's concentration, well, brain-work ..."

There was nothing sarcastic about the modesty in the voice.

A pause.

"To invent things like that, I bet you have to have a bit of brain!"

"Yes . . . or else be cracked."

They were still talking about the gas. The hammering of the guns drowned the whispered conversation in the trench, and my father could make out nothing more until a voice shouted out to God knows whom, to itself perhaps:

"If the English didn't have their colonies, they'd be the weakest country in the world!"

No one answered. Another voice went on with another private conversation:

"The women work on the sorting; before, it used to be in the pit, now it's at the surface, there's a conveyor-belt. But when you're married, you can't work in the mine any more."

"A miner isn't allowed to be married?"

"Not the men: the women. A married woman isn't allowed into the works. That's final."

Silence again. The darkness, like the darkness in mines, the heavy gunfire and the distant burst of the shells.

"And you know, in the shafts, in the galleries, you always work starkers, just your pants. You don't have to bother about eye-shadow! But coal-dust, it's good for the skin . . . . Your lamp, it's your guardian angel. Without your lamp, you're done for."

In spite of the shafts of light from the observation-holes, the magical respect with which the word "lamp" had been uttered was in keeping with the darkness of the trench.

"There's an inspection every week—talk about a kit-check. I had a litle tart, a pretty little tart; she used to polish my lamp for me every day."

The soldier was speaking in a whisper, with great affection. My father could see nothing in front of him: a man who was reminded of love when he thought of a miner's lamp and a naked torso covered in coal-dust . . .

Another voice, closer, drowned the first one:

" . . . the chap had asked specially for the captain's report so as to go on leave; he'd been on the western front, then landed up here, and he hadn't had one day's C.B.! And he had a kid of five. At five, kids start to cotton on . . . Well, he got his pass, goes back, and the kid says: 'Where are you going to sleep?' 'Where d'you think?' he says; 'in bed!' 'I see,' says the brat, 'then the Swiss can't come?' Imagine, there'd been a Swiss sleeping with his old woman every night!"

"What happened then?"

"Well, nothing. He didn't exactly jump for joy . . . but he let it go on, because of the kid."

For a few seconds the fury of the guns filled the trench.

"I knew a chap who went on leave without being able to let his people know. It was night time, he knocked: no answer. And he knew his old woman was there all right! He went on knocking nearly all night. She didn't answer. She didn't want to. Then he understood. He went back to the squadron, and then he hung himself."

There was something extraordinary, disturbing, about

142

hearing someone talk about suicide while waiting for an attack.

"I also knew a chap who hung himself. But this chap was a dirty sod. He was an old lag, or something, and had been inside for five years. It happened with a couple of girls, fifteen or sixteen they were, imagine! Well, one fine day they're both in pod. He'd started to go with one of them, then with the other. And then the mother was in pod as well. The kids were born with a fortnight and three weeks between them, and then the farmer—they were a farmer's daughters—decided to run him in. So this chap, instead of appearing in court, he went home, and then he hung himself. Just like that, with his belt, from the bed-post. And yet it was just an ordinary bed. . . ."

Listening in this live darkness, my father was conscious for the first time of the people of Germany. Or perhaps just of people: men. A voice close to the darkness of primitive man, like these silhouettes barely visible in the shadows. His relationship with the men had always been of the falsest kind, the relationship between an officer and men who were not in his command; for a year he had been rubbing shoulders with a world which he thought he knew—as though one could know men simply by being a man . . . He knew what these men had learnt at school, but not what they had forgotten since.

"I don't believe *The Limping Messenger*, but it did say: 'When the harvest is a bad one and the servants' names begin with the same letter as the Master's, there will be war.' "

"Hindenburg . . ."

No one mentioned the name "Hohenzollern", which they were all thinking about. My father knew *The Limping Messenger*, one of those old almanacks published in Strasbourg. "When the harvest is a bad one . . ." The ageless peasant connection between the unpredictable harvest and man's unpredictable destiny.

"Which side wins, in the prophecy? Do we?"

Guns in the silence.

"I don't know."

A few seconds more of gunfire.

"I'll tell you what we ought to do," yelled one of the ghosts in the cloth-covered helmets; "when we get over there, eh, to Petersburg, to Paris, well, we ought to mobilise all the doctors, all the vets, all that lot! And then, the others, we'd castrate them! Like the Colonel said: 'Once and for all.' It's not humanitarian, perhaps, but that way we'd finish them once and for all, and without killing any one!"

"Poor bloody fool! There's nothing wrong with the Russian or the Frenchman or the German," said another voice, as though stating a basic truth; "it's just mankind in general!"

One could picture the raised finger, the tell-tale attitude; my father realised that popular stupidity is a parody of popular wisdom in the same way that intellectual stupidity is a parody of intellectual wisdom. But he remembered one voice, almost like this one, however, which, shortly after he had started listening, had said: "Life . . . As long as you're young, you believe there are great people. So you wait. Then, afterwards, you start to grow old. You realise it's not true. There are no great people. There never have been. Never!"

Further off, they were saying:

"No, no: by the time we got there, they'd already been raped by the Cossacks and the Austrians, they weren't even struggling any more . . ."

The Professor now remained crouched over the observation-hole like a great daddy-long-legs, his feet tucked up in the muffler in which he was doing his best to smother himself. But several of the soldiers who were not wearing shirts had unbuttoned their tunics.

"You don't know the Lutheran cross?" said a hoarse voice, in answer not to the castrater, but to a question my father had not heard. "What do you know then?"

A different voice from the ones he had heard up to now —still common, but restrained, and one in which he could sense the hint of a smile. On someone's chest, close to him, a ray of light was shining with the brilliance of an electric bulb, on the arms of a cross and the luminous bead of the Huguenot dove. The same voice again answered a question which my father could not quite hear:

"I'm not a believer, but I like to go to church from time to time. So as to be alone. In certain circumstances . . ."

"Which ones?"

"I don't know. When I'm unhappy. Or when I want to remember . . ."

The speakers moved off. Quite a time passed in relative silence; the guns were now firing only at rare intervals.

The footsteps of the men he had just heard—N.C.O.s—
brought them back to him.

"There's always the moral problem when it comes to
volunteers. Look: I needed three of them a little while ago,
and this gas business can always be . . . a bit tricky. I took
the three nicest chaps. Why? Because they wanted to
come, they were keen on it, I wanted to be nice to them.
As for pleasing them, I've probably condemned them to
death. And I should have chosen the ones whose death,
in any case, would matter least."

"And how do you solve it, this moral problem?"

My father could not hear the answer: a shrug, probably.

"Now, when I was still working in the Ruhr, we got
into a shaft where there'd been a firedamp explosion some
time before. There was a workman there, like he was alive,
with his pick at arm's length, and the horse behind him,
which still looked as if it was pulling the skip. It was the
gas had preserved them, but the air got in with us. In less
than ten minutes, pfutt! the chap and the nag were both
dust!"

An unusually violent uproar stirred the darkness, and
out of it came:

"Gas, I'll tell you what it does . . ."

It was the low, measured voice of people in face of a
mystery, the voice which makes one suspect how infantile
the old-time wizards' voices probably were:

"Gas, I'll tell you: the chap who gets it, eh, he's struck
still. Rooted to the spot . . . he can't move any more. Stays
just as he was when he got it, just the same. Chaps playing
cards, for instance . . ."

"Before you know it, you're dead!"

"And if the wind changes?"

The guns had stopped firing. The sun on the ground over there shone with the same brilliance on the wide bend of the river as it did in the days of peace.

"Do they know they're going into the attack behind gas?" the Professor's voice broke in behind my father.

"The command has organised the attack," an N.C.O.'s voice shouted authoritatively, as though answering the Professor and the soldiers at the same time.

"That's what they say," an anonymous voice weakly replied.

That was all, until a new gas-expert chimed in.

"They tried it out on the western front. When it was on them, the French were caught off their guard, all the grave-diggers were taking the dead to a cemetery, next to the Death House. There they stuck, with their feet turned up, with the dead in the blankets, imagine! Just like dead men in a shop-window."

"Here, I say. Just 'cause you're a grave-digger, you don't have to feed us that sort of balls."

"With their feet turned up, I tell you, you silly sod!"

"Oh, cut it out!"

"I tell you, that's how they were!"

They did not know that in France Death Houses did not exist. They raised their voices more and more, following the recognised method of popular argument: saying the same thing over and over again in a louder and louder voice. These moments, when so many voices adopted the same rhythm, the same clumsiness and the same anger in order to discuss things as different as Frederick II and gas, succeeded each other in the dark underground like the pulsating of blood.

"Now look here, I know what I'm talking about when I tell you about the west: I've got a cousin who went to Nancy. Even to Rheims!"

"So what? My brother's been to Paris!"

"Paris?" said another voice professorially. "Paris isn't France: you'd soon realise it's different. On its own."

"Put a sock in it!" shouted a third voice.

For the time being they were not interested in Paris. They were interested in one thing only: gas.

"A crossing-sweeper, dead in his tracks, with his broom upside down, can you see it?"

"A pig being killed, the knife sticks in his guts; but with this lark there's not a squeal out of him!"

Were these men that were talking, or professions?

"No, but joking apart, doesn't the river stop as well, sometimes?"

"I say, you chaps! This lark, they could always go in for it, the officers, to make us do arms drill: the rifle's chucked up, it can't come down! Very funny!"

"Come to that, the shells, they stick up there and won't come down! Too fed up!"

But joking was only a means of dreaming without shame. Each one saw life suddenly arrested—not so much the enemy's life as his own.

"The accountant who can't finish his sum . . ." mumbled a shy voice. Appearing and disappearing in the shafts of light that still shook with the deep thunder of our guns, they all pursued the same mad game till it turned into a shindy in which obscene, scatalogical fancies played a leading part. When this petered out, the words became clear again:

"They're not as wonderful as you think, these things, gas, and machines. Those people don't know about animals. If you make a slit in a mule's nose, it can't bray any more. You can't hear it. D'you realise what you could do with mules like that—like having cavalry the others couldn't hear?"

The guns still stirred the beams of light. My father could not stop looking at his watch, as though he knew what time he was waiting for.

"The French are mobilising kids of seventeen. Half of them desert."

"They'll have a revolution; it's a country that always has a revolution."

"Is the cholera over in London? When we have only one front . . ."

But the containers were too close to lift the haunting obsession of gas.

"All the same, can you see it, a farrier with his hammer in the air above the anvil, not moving! It's balls, that sort of thing, the hammer'd come down, seeing it's so heavy."

"And the electric light, that's bound to stay on."

My father was reminded of the town in *The Thousand and One Nights*, where every human gesture, the life of flowers, the flames of a lamp, were arrested by the Angel of Death . . . He was here, quite close, in the container-heads. But the passage of time also leads so certainly to death, that the old dream of fate being arrested kept recurring as though it was the secret of the world, lurking in these men with their spiked helmets covered with grey cloth, as it had once lurked beneath the helms of Saladin's soldiers. In this mushroom-bed smell my father saw, for a split second, the petrified gestures of the mythological blacksmiths under light for ever forgotten—a light scarcely dimmed by the passage of fleeting human wills, fleeting as the war and as the German army. The man who had just mentioned the electric light, one of the poorest soldiers, with the face of an hereditary alcoholic, came into a beam of sunlight to rummage in a tiny little bag he had taken out of his pack, a ridiculous doll's bag, as though that too bore the stamp of his poverty. The darkness was once again alive with voices, unconcerned voices, venerable voices, professional voices—as though only their professions lived on inside these impersonal, provisional men. Their pitch varied, but their tone remained the same, very old, enveloped in the past like the shadows in this trench—the same resignation, the same false note of authority, the same absurd opinions and the same experiences, the same inexhaustible cheerfulness, and these arguments consisting of protests that grew more and more violent, as though these voices in the dark had never even managed to individualise their anger.

My father turned back to the parapet, but he was still listening. A few roofs sparkled in the sun. There was something unbearable about this waiting.

But it had to be borne, and time was once again military time, transparent time which depends only on orders from above—like death. Dazzling shafts of light from the rising sun bespattered the legs gloomily pacing the trench, making the boots suddenly gleam. Under one of the shafts a pack of tarot cards was spread out, clear against the charred ground; from time to time a hand would pick out a card, with a murmur of effort, striving to forecast a life. In the shadows peopled with gliding figures this disembodied hand seemed to be running over the cards of all eternity.

After a fresh silence, a voice, quite close to my father, whispered in a tone of affectionate apology: "It wasn't for her looks I married her."

One of the soldiers, or one of the N.C.O.s, was showing someone else a photograph. In the darkness his words had a mysterious intensity. The two men were quite close, but where? Near the observation-holes no one was showing anyone anything. Under the nearest one a good-looking boy sat reading. Was it he who had just spoken? He had not moved. Not once, since my father had been listening, had he turned to any friend, and not once had he looked outside. The look-out man was on the look-out, and this lad, crouching over his machine-gun in the light coming through the hole, was reading. What on earth could he be reading like this?

Two figures walked by, vaguely outlined against a faint halo: the photograph was illuminated by the small flame of a lighter. With the same tender resignation another voice, the hoarse voice that had said: "I go to church when I want to remember," now replied:

"Well, you know, my wife's not much to look at either."

How low the roof of the dug-out is! The grave-digger came back.

"... but you see, Mr. Kapp, they found a dog. It was all right for us to keep it, wasn't it, since it hadn't been paid for! My wife called it Peterl, almost like my own name. My kid had never been able to say her father's name. Well, Mr. Kapp, believe it or not, ever since the dog's been there, the kid says 'Peter' just like anyone else!"

The voice became bitter.

"She didn't manage to do it for me. Still, it's something all the same."

He came into the light. A small, oldish fellow, moving like a crazy rabbit, he was swinging the covered helmet he held in his left hand by its chin-strap. His shaven pate still had a small lock of fair hair on it, like a Moslem's. For he was a joker, this chap. He stroked his lock and went on in a sad voice with the story about the dog.

Still listening, my father turned back to the observation-hole. Under the high clouds hanging over the Russian lines a flight of birds was sweeping down towards the Vistula. Bird life went on, and the life of fir-trees, and all the life of the earth.

"It's something all the same," the grave-digger was saying in a lower key, and his words were lost in the general murmur.

Up there birds were gliding past, and in the swarming semi-darkness my father listened to the voice of the only species that has learnt—and learnt so badly—that it can die.

Against the green background already yellowed by summer, great waves of umbels heaved in the wind. The

first-line trenches were a little further down—not very far
—above those white half-withered flowers which in the
distance were transformed by the wind into long floral
patterns, but which in front of the observation-holes
were shaken in wild confusion. Beyond this improbable
thrust-and-parry the road could be seen, which down
there ran alongside the river; then the Russian slope, so
peaceful that the barbed-wire entanglement looked like
pastureland fences. Not a single man, not a single animal
was visible. The guns had stopped firing. The radiance of
this valley was inseparable from the distant song of larks,
the sound of crickets, living noises; and to these was due
the silence that covered everything like the clear pale sky,
rather than to the last echo of shellbursts, which was the
the war.

A long cloud of dust was floating in the sunshine. Not
feathering out like the dust in the wake of a car, but
uniformly thick and tall, like a wall. It went on growing
although no motor could be heard. The road disappeared
completely: the gas-launching had begun.

In the dug-out, there was a rush for the parapets. The
sheet of gas went on growing, swamping the parallel
trunks of the apple-trees to the same height, then their
branches. Soon the bottom of the valley was only a
yellow fog, reddening along the sides of the fields and the
green fir-trees, from which there protruded a single
absurd, ghostly shape, a tall telegraph pole.

Slowly the sheet of gas spread out to the depth of half
a mile, engulfing the valley completely, moving towards
the Russian advanced position that seemed the closest. It

curled into a wood, at the foot of the hill which neither the
Russians nor the Germans had wanted to occupy; it
blanketed the bottom of the fir-trees without reaching up
to the top of them, reappeared further on, so that jagged
saw-tooth ridges stood out against the background of fog,
as in a Japanese print. Then it continued its sluggish
ascent, combining in a single colour-scheme of red and
yellow the fields that rolled down in strips towards the
trenches, the purple fields of clover, the rye, and the huge
squares of bare ground spotted with ricks; and finally,
at the highest point, near the Russian trenches, the copses
growing thicker and thicker, and the stretch of forest
carved into clearings which the artillery had pounded.
Nothing moved in it.

All of a sudden something darted out of the Russian
lines in the direction of the gas. My father at once took up
his binoculars: a horse, which appeared small, even in the
lenses. How much faster the gas seemed to be moving
now that it was approaching the trenches! Riderless,
the horse charged towards it, with the rhythmic movement of galloping seen from a distance. It stopped,
turned about, then dashed off to the left, and the sound
of hooves on a road reached the dug-out across the ground,
surprisingly clear, much closer than that tiny horse tossed
into space. It stopped again. Everyone was watching it as
though it was the Russian Army itself. A whinny came
across the valley, carried from a long way off on the wind.
Through the binoculars it seemed that the horse had
whinnied, its head in the air, like a dog howling. It gal-
loped off again, darted straight into the gas. Its hooves

could no longer be heard, and in a few seconds it was swallowed up in the vast silence.

Would it re-emerge, as if from underwater, at some point on the reddish fringe? All eyes were on it, scanning it from end to end, and the sheet now seemed less immense against the huge contours of the hillside. The horse did not reappear; every second of waiting was like a second of the horse's agony, and the ceaseless, creeping advance of the gas, which seemed bound to continue up to the ends of the earth, the dying whinny, the almost clear-cut edges of the sheet, began to give this commonplace fog the look of a war machine. And the non-appearance and silence of the Russians was linked up with its stealthy advance.

Had they evacuated their positions? Even with binoculars it was difficult to judge the moment when the gas would reach their trenches. Soon they would be submerged; and, apart from that strange horse whinnying out there in the sun before dashing headlong as though for a sacrifice, nothing came out of them. It was impossible that they should be already evacuated: the Russians had never dug long connecting galleries; the open space behind their lines was over half a mile deep and there was no one moving in it. At the bottom of the valley, the small clump of fir trees and the telegraph pole with its insulators had disappeared in the gathering gas; half-way up, a few tree tops still protruded. The tufts of grass and the slender thistles concealing the observation-holes were silhouetted against the milky background of the gas. The Professor, his nose twitching between the two eyepieces of his binoculars, was leaning on my father with all his weight.

For a second the latter believed the Russians must have been warned. Had they found a means of stopping the gas, which seemed to be disappearing on the very edge of their parapets? When the wind gathered it up in sufficient quantity, the gas moved on as though it had sprung over them. But everyone was hoping so fervently for it to move on, and its advance seemed so slow, that it was already two hundred yards beyond the trenches before anyone was confident that it had reached them.

The further it advanced, the slower it moved. If the Russians were there, what was happening inside that silent fog?

"The opaque cornea first goes blue, the breath starts to come in hisses, the pupil—it's really very odd!—goes almost black. No Russian will be able to bear the pain...."

Was that going on inside that fog where nothing moved? It was still advancing with the twisting movements of a prehistoric saurian, as though it would never stop while it still remained on earth.

"And when our troops get there," Wurtz asked, "there won't be any more gas in the trenches?"

"Nothing to worry about," the Professor answered sharply; "the gas will be cleared, and there's always the ambulance. And besides, I . . ."

His sentence was cut short by a frenzied renewal of the Russian guns firing all at once. What telephone message had they received from the trenches? They were now pounding the gas with the same breathless fury as they would have used to check an onslaught. The shells were bursting spasmodically, red and angry on the sheet which had gone yellow again; when they slashed at the edges of it, the shreds round it shifted a little quicker than the yellowish mass itself, without, however, coming apart from it completely. And the sheet which stirred in the red glare, like a river in the beams of a setting sun, pushed forward with its leisurely, scourge-like advance, no longer looking like a fog, but transformed into what it really was: poison gas.

As suddenly as it had started, the Russian artillery stopped.

"Remember now," a commanding voice immediately shouted in the dug-out, "anyone feeling a symptom of poisoning withdraws at once to the ambulance. Is that clear? Taste of bitter almonds, breath hissing . . . Quite clear?"

The company lined up in the starting-off trench. To follow them there, my father and his two companions crossed the dug-out. The young soldier who had been reading by the parapet had forgotten his book: it was *The Adventures of Three Boy Scouts*. And on the ground, in a corner—forgetfulness or superstition—the fortune-teller had left his pack of cards spread out, the fate of one of these men who were moving off in front of us in this clash of water-bottles, braced packs, buckles and metalwork.

Behind the front lines the medical staff was in attendance. All the M.O.s were there; there was not one ambulance —there were four.

When my father and his companions reached the front-line observation-post, the gas had disappeared over the far side of the ridge; only the Japanese mist remained at

the bottom of the valley, and the sinister blackish remains
of everything it had touched, as though it had left in its
wake a huge slice of winter under the radiant sky. Still no
activity from the Russian trenches.

The first-line infantry, which had started much earlier,
was crossing the river. My father could see it quite
clearly—and no doubt the Russians could as well. Between the vast, stagnant banks of the river, men were
creeping forward as though through a marsh, separating,
joining up again. At the top of the fir-trees the wind
was blowing shreds of greenish cloud about. With the
river behind them, the units, without halting their advance,
took up battle formation.

The green silhouettes and cloth-covered helmets of the
132nd were converging on a large hollow field. Although
the manoeuvre which my father and his companions were
watching was taking place in folds of ground invisible to
the enemy, they suddenly felt convinced that the German
troops were just as vulnerable as though the Russians
were able to see them as they could. All this silence, this
whole valley sparkling around the sinister stain, was a
trap. The Professor wanted to speak to Wurtz, but
stopped: he was panting. Everyone was waiting on tenterhooks for the first shell to announce the renewed barrage
of the Russian artillery, the ranging shots behind, then in
front, and the pounding of the halted troops.

The companies reformed but stopped advancing.

Miner for whom the lamp was a guardian angel, N.C.O.
who went to church in order to remember, grave-digger
whose child had only learnt his Christian name because of

the dog, fitter, accountant, hairdresser, pig-killer, crossing-sweeper, reader of *The Adventures of Three Boy Scouts*, the man who had not married his wife for her looks, and the man whose wife was not much to look at either, men like so many others, between all the dead men and the men who had been killed! And with them would die their pathetic impersonal feelings, their destiny which had tried to find its way into those tarot-cards on which a kindly sunbeam was now playing; their resignation born of experience, as though so many common graves had been dug and scattered only to end up as an example of a petty wisdom: "He let it go on, because of the kid"; and their castration-mania at an end like the last undertow of the Golden Age, hand-in-hand with their dreams emerging from so far back in the past, the smithies with their hammers arrested in mid-air like the hammers of subterranean smithies lost in the depths of the earth's memory. High above, the great flight of birds was sweeping on; and underneath, the human species flattened on those livid fields, waiting for the pounding from the Russians, had the same complex harmony as a summer night, the harmony of distant cries, dreams, presences, of the penetrating smell of trees and cut corn, of restless sleep on the face of the earth under the immense, unstirring sky.

3

THE ENEMY artillery still did not fire. The troops gradually forsook their cover, advanced on the trenches. My father and his companions moved up past the first lines, across a wood: when they came out into the open again, the soldiers were approaching the Russian lines.

In his binoculars my father picked up the 132nd which was now among the leading companies. Under their spiked, cloth-covered helmets, like Saracens' helms, the rows of little bodies concealed the barbed-wire fence; the jostling advance stopped, the human spots began to squirm in and out of the wire network, to kick about in it like spiders in an invisible web, for my father could see only the posts. The stubborn advance which had been slowed down by distance, like the advance of the gas, gave way to a static puppet-show, a sinister ballet which had no end. At last, they all plunged into the Russian trench.

No: some of them remained on the barbed wire. They in their turn fell, and fresh companies came up, dangled on the wire, dived in. Only the wind could be heard, and on the whole battle-field not a man could be seen any more. There was no more war, no more attack, no more trenches, only the dazzling sun on the broad peasant landscape, on the wooden town still intact over there with its steeple. But neither my father nor Wurtz took their eyes off the vague line of Russian trenches into which the infantry had just plunged—where perhaps the fate of this war was now being decided.

The Professor seemed to be stuck fast in the eye-pieces of his binoculars, which were shaking. The troops had been ordered to push on towards the second enemy lines, then occupy as quickly as possible a group of copses behind the ridge which now concealed the advance of the gas; but not one of the soldiers reappeared.

"They could not have been gassed themselves?" my father at last asked.

The Professor shrugged his shoulders violently, making his binoculars shake still more:

"They've been told not to stay there! They've been ordered not to stay there! If they spend all their lives there, of course . . ."

He let go of his binoculars with his left hand, caught hold of my father's arm with his fingers. A man in shirt sleeves had just come out of the trench.

The white shape moved forward a little. What an extraordinary walk: a man over six feet tall, with tiny, almost horizontal head and shoulders. He stopped, fell down. There was another man with him. From one end of the trench to the other, men in shirt-sleeves were emerging, white spots distinct in spite of the distance. All over-tall, tottering like fair-ground giants with over-tall heads that were tottering too, on the end of a hidden broomstick. Why the devil had the soldiers taken off their tunics?

Several fair-ground giants fell apart. The half of the body in shirt-sleeves dropped off, the other, the lower half of the body, went on walking. They were made of two men, one carrying the other. Were there already so many casualties? Was there any gas left in the bottom of the trench? And still this silence in the wind.

Some soldiers were coming back through the barbed-wire, moving with the same gait, like spiders. Unerringly they cut their way through.

Not one of them was advancing towards the Russian second lines.

The soldiers in green lifted those with the white spots on to their shoulders again, and the limping procession ploughed through the openings in the wire.

The assault wave was not launching itself at the Russians—it was coming back.

Along the whole line—a confused swarm round the soldiers who were carrying the white spots like ants carrying their eggs—the troops were flooding back through the openings made by the wire-cutters. They were evacuating the Russian position. In this silence, without a gun shot. Without a rifle shot.

The Professor dropped his binoculars, which were slung round his neck on a cord, and ran forward, his muffler flying.

On my father's left there was a horse: he took it and dashed forward. The companies now retreating in disorder disappeared and reappeared, closer and closer as the galloping horse brought him nearer and nearer. At length my father crossed the path of two soldiers who looked at him without seeing him. They saw nothing. They were running.

"What are the Russians up to?"

He yelled, but they did not hear him: the only human faculty they still retained was the ability to run. They disappeared under the trees. His horse was chafing from time to time, whinnying like the one that had thrown itself into the gas. At last a soldier of the 132nd appeared. He too was running, his helmet off, a lock of hair (was it the grave-digger?) flapping in all directions in the wind, like an absurd spark of fire above his terrified face. My father set his horse across his path.

"Here, what are the Russians up to?" he shouted again.

The man looked at him as though he understood and, with frantic waving of his arms and head, answered:

"We can't! We simply can't!"

"You can't what? And your weapons? Why . . ."

"We can't! We . . ."

He began to yell "no", with his hands, his shoulders, his head. He was suffocating. With both arms outstretched in the gesture of a speaker addressing an audience, his forelock tossed in all directions by the wind, he pointed furiously to the flesh-coloured clover thick with flowers in which they were standing, as though inveighing against this pink fleece within the four dark-green walls of the trees. He looked at my father again with an expression of unutterable horror and, just as the latter was going to speak, the man rushed furiously away. My father put his horse into a gallop, and as it came thundering out of the wood, it skidded for five yards, legs stiff, and pitched him off into the bushes. When he could look up again, the horse was still in the rigid, terrified pose of a statue; life ebbed back into its lips which curled back from its teeth, then suddenly seethed through its body, from its ears to its spine, and it bolted hysterically into the forest. My father was in front of the ground over which the gas had spread.

He began to rub his knee-cap, still looking straight in front of him, waiting for the arrival of his own men or the Russians; his fingers came up against something repulsive like tufts of dead hair, spiders' webs, dust-fuzz. His boot had scraped the ground for nearly a yard, filling the space between leather and knee with the clover and umbels of wild carrot growing beside the bushes: black, sticky, as though churned up from the depths of some foul mud. The flowers were almost intact in shape: exactly what corpses are to living bodies. His hand drew back with the same disgust that life feels for carrion. In the open field in front of him, over a distance of more than three hundred yards, the gas had left not an inch of life. On the tufts of grass, flattened where the wind had made scythe-like patterns on them, the sun was shining with the same dim light as it sheds on coal. A few rows of apple trees were left standing, decomposed, and hanging like moss-covered trees, their dung-coloured leaves plastered against the dead-looking branches. Apple trees, pruned by man, killed like men: more dead than the other trees, because fertile. All the grass underneath them was black, a black never seen before. Black the trees enclosing the horizon, and slimy, too; dead the woods across which some shapes of German soldiers were now moving, plunging deeper into them on seeing my father get up. Dead the grass, dead the leaves; dead the earth on which the galloping hooves of the bolting horse were vanishing into the wind.

The only things still standing between the apple trees were the clumps of thistles, whose heads, prickles and leaves had turned the same rusty colour as a flower on the point of falling into dust, while their stems had taken on the repulsive whiteness of anatomical specimens. The slimy field lay at right angles between two walls of forest, its two branches as deep as the rides of a park. Although wounded in the knee, my father was able to walk; he trailed behind him huge clods of earth which grew heavier and heavier. The sound of his horse galloping was drowned in the noise of the wind, and in front of him another horse with legs bunched up as in a race-course snapshot had collapsed, no doubt the one that had charged into the gas: not yet stiff, grey eyes wide open, coat rotting like the grass and the leaves, every muscle convulsed. There were mullein herbs growing round it, their tapering heads rust-red like the thistles, but all their leaves shrivelled; on one of them a swarm of dead bees had stuck, like the grains on a head of corn. Beyond the deep entrance of this valley of death, beyond the distant line of telegraph poles and wires, the wind was chasing clouds high up in the birdless sky.

My father was moving heavily, but he was moving. Isolated in this wilderness, as though guarding the gassed horse, was a dead tree; not contaminated by the gas, but with every branch clear-cut, sharply outlined, ossified, thrusting upwards tragically like any other dead tree on earth. And this tree which had been petrified for so many years, seemed, in this universal putrefaction, to be the last remnant of life. A magpie flew slowly by, its white feathers standing out in its black wings; and fell like a bird made of rags.

My father at last reached the far side of the forest. It was no longer a question of walking through foulness, but of plunging right into it. The undergrowth of bramble and double hawthorn was mowed down, shining livid-red, a kind of burst-animal colour that turns to black at a distance of twenty yards. But the brambles no longer caught hold of him: with the disturbing sensation of having recovered his strength my father went forward, meeting no resistance as he pushed through the thorny barricade which gave way under his knees, under his shoulders, under his stomach. The only things that still pricked him were the long thorns of acacia whose branches did not snap at the first touch; their leaves seemed to be only beginning to wither, nipped by an early autumn. Above his head, all the different leaves which now looked alike— oak, beech, larch, poplar—hung down like boiled lettuce, with an occasional spider dead in the centre of its web in which there sparkled a greenish dew. Matted ivy clung to the suppurating tree-trunks. At each step, a bitter-sweet smell rose from the crushed bushes, no doubt the smell of gas. Suddenly four soldiers appeared, covered in leaves: the upper leaves—which the gas had hardly touched— but just enough for the high wind to snatch them off like dead leaves—clung to the vegetation sticking to their uniforms. They were walking one behind the other, without looking at each other; it was hardly possible to walk two abreast along this path. My father barred their way, but he had lost the authority with which he had tried to stop the grave-digger; and he was no longer on horseback. They were just as horrified as he was by these leaves, these suppurating tree-trunks, decomposing but still upright. The first one, dull faced, with heavy eyelids, halted less than a yard away.

"It's nothing to do with me," he said through clenched teeth, looking at everything except my father, with a hunted look; "not with me, nothing to do with me!"

And he walked off through the trees, to the left, wallowing in the slime. The second and third went past side by side, as though they were both supporting each other against my father. One of them shouted in his face:

"No, no, old boy, no!" as though fed up with a long speech (perhaps the speech he had been hearing from every one of his officers ever since the beginning of the war). The other was laughing hysterically.

"Good God! Are there any casualties?" my father was thinking. The soldier laughed still more and went on; my father realised that he had said nothing. The last one, rising to his full height, shook his head, hesitated, stamped his foot, making the dead leaves sticking to his greatcoat shower down.

"Because I, Sir, have something to tell you!"

Whereupon, amazed at hearing his voice in the silence, he plunged like the others into the matted thickets.

Beyond the curtain of trees, the tops of some of the tallest of them still green in the wind above these infernal woods, my father could see the troops collapsing on the steep slope, hundreds of men in shirt-sleeves being carried by others. Limping, taking short cuts, he plunged into the foul trees again. Plastered with leaves, the soldiers he met in their flight all looked at him with the same wild expression of hate, as though he had been responsible for an ambush, and they refused to answer him. One of them, coming quite close, glanced behind him stealthily, with a nervous jerk of the head. He was running away, but not from fear. Never had my father seen such an expression on anyone's face; with delirious certainty he felt it was a look of remorse. But remorse for what?

The light above the deep gullies outlined in silhouette, as on a sky-line, the sordid world of the liquefied forest. Out of the nearest one, pushed from below, a body appeared, again in shirt-sleeves, its arms hanging as in a "Descent from the Cross". Then the man who was carrying it. The first German gas casualty. My father broke into a run, fell down again, ran on; the pain in his knee had died down.

It was not a German, it was a Russian.

But the man carrying him was certainly a German. He watched my father approaching with the same expression of hate as the others.

"What is it? What's happened? What? What?"

The German had the face of an old, old peasant. He stood there, two yards off, his legs braced under the load, covered by this big body spattered with thrown-up leaves; his furrowed brow grew darker still. He gave my father a sidelong glance, as hunted game do. Carrying the Russian on his shoulders, he had thrown his rifle away. My father thought he had just shouted, and realised that for the second time he had not uttered a word.

"The ambulance," said the man at last, threateningly through clenched teeth.

"But Christ Almighty, what's happened?"

My father had just recovered his voice.

"Where they've got some medical stuff!"

The man's forehead clouded more and more. He seemed far older than my father who could feel, just as though this soldier had shouted it out, how much he despised him for his obvious youth. The soldier gave a heave of his chest, carefully so as not to drop the body, yet brutally as though he wanted to throw the Russian's face into my father's face. The thrust of his shoulders jerked the hanging head which twisted round to disclose, instead of his tobacco-coloured hair, the face of the man who had been gassed—a ghastly face. The same bitter-sweet smell rose from his greatcoat as from the crushed branches. In the German's every moment, in the way he held the body, there was a pathetic, clumsy comradeship.

"Must do something," he said, a little less threateningly.

The Russian's lips and eyes showed purple in his grey skin. His nails were scratching at his shirt, trying to tear it apart, without being able to get hold of it. Under the sinister trees from which the leaves kept falling, the light marbled the great expanse of forest which was leaden with decomposition; the wind rippled the stagnant surface of a marsh close by, which was bordered with stiff mould like watercress—the only green thing in the whole forest—and in it, rolling from one little island of firm ground to the other, was the swollen body of a squirrel, its tail limp. Without another word the man stumbled off, like the others.

My father pushed forward. He had to get out of this wood where he would find out nothing, where nothing human existed or could exist. The sunlit gap of the ravine round which he was tottering gave a Chinese-ink precision to the rags of the lower branches, to the leaves

falling in clouds like hanging capes, to the tentacles clinging to the tree-trunks, to this marsh-bottom world. But
it was not only the gap of the ravine, it was the closeness
of its edge that caused all these trunks covered in dead
seaweed to emerge one after the other out of the powdery
mist; a mist full of the sparkle of June in the falling
wind, which endowed this dreary, drowned forest with the
great peace of summer undergrowth. My father had not
looked at the Russian's face for more than five seconds.
For over a year he had again seen his share of wounded
and dead, the stiffness of the first corpses under their
blankets, and the coal-black faces on the barbed-wire
entanglements; but no dead man's face would ever make
him forget those terrible features.

What he was coming to was not a clearing, but yet
another open field walled in by the slimy trees; the
tortured grass disclosed countless little spiders' webs,
intact, sparkling with a poisonous dew; in the shimmering
light they twinkled from one end of the field to the other,
as though carpeting it with flowers. And through all
this nauseating brilliance, a tiny speck of light shone
out, like a window which a beam from the setting sun
suddenly causes to flash out from a town in the haze
of sunset. It was shining on the chest of a soldier bent
under the weight of a Russian: a pendant in the triangle
of his shirt which was open to the waist, and the man
was now close enough for my father to make out the
dove and crucifix, the double bead of the Huguenot
cross; in this madness he looked on that little cross as
the face of a friend.

This "good dog" face lashed by curly hair which the wind flattened along its nose, helmetless, bore no resemblance to the face glimpsed in the dug-out. The soldier waited, eyelids fluttering, straightened his back, slowly so as not to drop the body, also so as to get rid of a painful cramp.

"It's a long way," he said.

He too was trying to be hostile, but as he gradually straightened his back, his face lit up with relief, and suddenly he smiled at the surrounding desolation. My father noticed his badges of rank:

"You're an N.C.O.? What . . . why . . .?"

The man instinctively nodded his head, and his neck being wedged under the Russian's body whose arms hung down on his right, his legs on his left, he winced, without the wince being able to wipe out the blank smile which was spreading with relief over his face.

"Why?" he repeated in bewilderment.

My father thought he recognised the hoarse voice in the trench: "There's the moral problem, with volunteers. . . ." Certainly not a peasant.

"But we can't leave them up there either."

Words he had heard before. To admit their pity, they spoke of it as a fatality. Obviously, it was to the Russians he was referring.

"Has there been an order to withdraw?"

The N.C.O. listened, his thick lips parted, trembling against a background of apple trees consumed by diseased mistletoe, still fluttering his eyelids violently.

"There aren't any orders any more," he said at last. Unable to make any gesture under the heavy body he was carrying, he shook his head as if to explain that orders had vanished forever, with the whole of the world.

"But what about the officers?" my father shouted.

"I don't know."

Even defiance seemed just a memory of the other world, useless.

"They're in the same boat. No, man wasn't born to rot!"

Behind him some soldiers were coming out of the wood opposite my father.

"There's nothing to be done," the N.C.O. went on. "You should have seen . . ."

What he remembered made him set off again in the direction of the ambulance.

"But seen what?"

"Christ, go and look!"

My father followed him, walking at his heels and waiting for him like a dog. His knee was beginning to hurt. The N.C.O. was panting under the weight of the body.

Once again the terrible face of the first gas casualty came to mind. And the horse's head. The two men walked on, leaves all over their faces, their boots sucking at the ground one after the other. "The Russians, there's not one of 'em left . . ." Another three or four paces in the wind. "And it's impossible."

Horror still lurked in his voice, horror that blew the men before it as this endless wind was blowing the rotten leaves.

"If war had to be like that . . ."

He stopped to get his breath. Whole leaves blew into his open mouth. He spat them out, as though he was trying to vomit but could not.

Parallel to their course, in front of them, two soldiers were coming out of the wood which they were skirting. They were carrying a Russian in a chair formed by their arms; they stopped, and bending down till their hands were on the slippery ground they laid down the body. They straightened up as though from sleep, with the same smile as the N.C.O., looking beyond the woods and the dead fields—to get to the ambulance, they had to go down towards the river—beyond the yellow sunflowers nodding in the wind; in the distance colours still existed, flowers, green and tawny patches of earth, the patterns made by the wind on the gleaming river and on the vast expanse of ground. The Russian, stretched out on his back between them, made an effort to turn on to his stomach and succeeded at last. The two Germans straightened up slowly, their knees still half bent, as amazed as my father to discover this valley of Promised Land. The N.C.O. said something through clenched teeth which was drowned in the noise of his boots squelching through the leaves.

"What?" my father asked. His companion grunted again. He wanted to point something out, but his fingers were engulfed in the greatcoat of the man he was carrying.

"This chap," he said at last, "he's in a bad way."

The high wind was blowing into the shirts of the two men who stood stupefied with relief; behind them the casualty was trying to crawl back to the Russian lines. Over a hundred yards separated him from the wood; with each effort he advanced a mocking six inches, then fell back; crawled forward again towards his trench, towards the narrow grave of gas in which his own side lay rotting. And the most inhuman thing was not this dying man crawling along, his arms up to the elbows in the mud, his eyes staring at the herbs sheathed in dead swarms; it was the silence.

The Germans noticed the Russian moving off. They took the two paces which separated him from them; one of them kicked him in the bottom, then they both hoisted him up on to their arms, and off they went.

My father went down behind them, going into the trees again. They disappeared. He should have been going up to the Russian lines, and with every step he was going further from them; his orders had been not to to leave the Professor; he had left him and was now coming back to the ambulance, contrary to the strict orders he had been given. He should have been helping his companion, who was panting with every step under the weight of the dying man, but he dared not look him in the face, dared not touch him. As crazed now as the troops, he kept going down, kept going down through the thickets, an absurd figure, arms dangling, looking with idiot's eyes at the dead birds lying on the mush that had once been moss. Yet the enemy trench was probably less than three hundred yards off. He kept on turning towards it, and with every step drew further away from it.

174

The path began to slant more steeply in the direction of the German positions. In the middle of it a man was leaping on all fours, with such spasmodic jerks that it seemed he was being bounced along. Naked. Two yards off, the apparition lifted its grey face and whiteless eyes, opened its epileptic mouth as though to scream; my father drew back. Mad with pain, moving like any madman, as though its body was now only possessed by torment, with a few frog-like leaps it plunged into the putrescence.

Then, in the prehistoric silence, there was a scream, a scream of utter agony which ended up in a mew. And my father once again heard the noise of dead wood being snapped.

Above the path there were some Russian greatcoats scattered all over the place, shirts hanging, as though carbonised, on the fantastic branches; but not a sign of an explosion. And close by, in a tiny clearing concealed behind a row of sunflowers, some thirty men lay crumbling in a T-shaped trench: an enemy advanced post.

All dead, more or less naked, scattered across a pile of tattered clothes, clutching each other in convulsive groups. The comic dreams in the dug-out, the dead quite still with their cards in the air! Feet were sticking out of this petrified swarm of dead bodies, big toes curled like fists. And what upset my father more than their lead-coloured eyes, more than those hands twisting in the empty air, was the absence of any wound.

The absence of blood.

Although his hands were still, his right shoulder was shaking. His muscles contracted as though his whole body was trying to roll up into a ball; his elbows pressed so violently into his ribs that he could hardly breathe. It was not paralysis in the face of danger, it was overwhelming panic; believers probably call such a visitation of fear "the presence of the Devil". The Spirit of Evil was stronger here than death, so strong that he felt compelled to find a Russian, any Russian who had not been killed, put him on his shoulders and save him.

Five or six of them lay scattered in the bushes, under a greatcoat caught up by its collar and swinging in this madness like someone hanged; my father threw himself on the first one, supported himself against the yielding brambles and got up with him. He was holding a pair of fists that were like knots. The man had been writhing among the sunflowers, and a bracelet of one of these huge flat flower-heads, decomposed by the gas and pierced through by a blow, like a cake, now encircled his arm. My father, his eyes shut tight, his whole body glued to this brother's body which protected him like a shield against all that he was running away from, kept mumbling endlessly: "Quickly, quickly", not knowing what he meant by this, and no longer even aware that he was walking.

As soon as the sunlight struck him despite his sealed eye-lids, he opened his eyes, and the whole of the top of the Russian slope came into sight: he had come back to the clearing. Those long spinnies on the side of the hill, corroded and blackened by a decisive autumn, killed by an unreturning force like the force of Creation, were nothing compared with the face of a single gas casualty: on these stretches of ground struck by a biblical curse, my father saw only the death of men. And yet—his eyes were gradually getting used to the light—he felt the dead blaze quicken with a secret life, felt it quiver as the jungle quivers when its animals converge on the water-points. In the distance he could see the small white patches of countless shirts moving in almost parallel lines; from every point of the forest, men carrying other men, their ranks broken and re-broken by the anthill confusion of their flight, were coming slowly down in the wind towards the clearing in which the silence was not broken by their footsteps. What these men were doing, my father now knew: not through a mental process but through the body under whose weight he kept sinking into the ground up to his calf. On the whole of the dark slope he could see their lines extending, stretching into the waste land, buried in the woods, compelled by the same solemn fatality as clouds on the highest mountains; and from the nearest edge, from which more men were ceaselessly emerging, they seemed to him to be fanning out under the dark trees as far as the Vistula and as far as the Baltic.

Gaping, released, he watched the assault of pity tumbling down towards the ambulances.

He realised that the man he was carrying was very heavy—and that he was dead. He opened both his hands; the corpse collapsed. He no longer needed to clasp a body to him in order to fight against inhumanity.

At the edge of the clearing the N.C.O., whom he had forgotten since leaving the trench, was still stumbling along with his Russian. Just as my father caught up with him, he asked him pitifully:

"What's so funny?"

My father was screaming with laughter. They walked on for a long time in the wind, which no doubt was still blowing the gas along on the other side of the ridge.

Although the vegetable matter lay dead on all sides, its shape was not all spoiled, and here and there brambles and ferns stood up, intact like the thistles, outlined above the slime-flattened grass. In the sheltered spots they were still left standing. But the leaves, now that the wind was less filled with them, were being blown about by the hundred like bits of burnt paper, and long brambles like cobwebs were ground to powder as they struck my father's tunic, falling to the ground without one of their thorns catching hold.

"What the hell?" the N.C.O. suddenly said in a strange, questioning voice. He stopped, the whole weight of his body on his left leg which was sunk into the turf. The few words he had spoken until then had been spoken to the wind; he had blurted them out, scarcely aware of my father's presence; this time he turned his face as well as the whole of the Russian's body towards him; and yet he was looking "inwards", with the blank eyes of someone on the watch for his own body.

"You, have you ever eaten bitter almonds?"

"What's the matter? Are you . . .?"

The obsession of being gassed had been haunting my father ever since he had got to the first field.

Testing his tongue and the roof of his mouth, the N.C.O. suddenly straightened up, releasing himself angrily from the Russian, and stood for a second, his arms outstretched in the brambles and ferns of the high wind, while the body he had been carrying tumbled down with a dull thud. The Russian came to; my father could hear his breath hissing horribly, could see his hand clutching the N.C.O.'s trouser-leg. The latter kicked himself free from the rotten tufts of grass, but the hand did not let go.

"I've got three children!" the Russian cried in German. His other hand was trying to tear at his shirt. "Got-three-children, three-children, three . . ."

From the tone of his voice it was impossible not to recognise the phrase he had learnt by heart, the magic words which he thought were bound to save him in the war. He suddenly repeated it, the words cut short by the hissing of punctured bellows, as though his lungs had been pierced; wild-eyed, the N.C.O. was gazing in any direction in which he could not see him, always furtively dragging away the leg which the other was still clasping.

"But I'm twenty-six years old!" he finally yelled.

The Russian did not understand. He was a man with almost white hair, with the coarse, unfinished features that Russians often have. His blue lips were moving—were talking; his blue eyes with their black pupils were watching. He did not let go of the trouser-leg.

The N.C.O. tore his boot free with a violent jerk which grazed the Russian's face, and rushed away to the ambulances as fast as he could. My father lifted the Russian on to his shoulders. His knee was hurting more and more; it became difficult to walk and carry a body at the same time. In front of him some figures were plunging into the bushes; like the N.C.O., like himself, they were moving towards a great glimmer of clearing from which a distant voice was carried on the wind:

". . . no good . . . the other one instead! Over here! Dark blue . . . at the end, on the left. . . ."

My father moved towards it, but could no longer run.

"It's madness! The worst thing possible! Blue . . . on the left. . . ."

At the bottom of the wood Wurtz and the captain of the 132nd were rallying the men, trying to organise the transport of the wounded to the ambulance. Medical orderlies with dazzling gas-masks were moving towards some bodies lying on the ground. The Professor, also covered with leaves, his muffler flying, his hat pushed back and his arms like windmill sails, was snuffling round Wurtz like a gun-dog, rushing off to the casualties, coming back to Wurtz. My father felt the same hatred for him as the soldiers had felt for himself when they had met him. The Professor recognised him, ran up to him:

"You see! You see! Absolutely decisive!" He yelled: "No, you fools!" then turned back to my father: "Those chaps over there," (my father could speak a few words of Russian) "tell them they mustn't!"

With dilated pupils he scanned the length and breadth of the field where the number of casualties was increasing.

"Yes, those fools drinking!"

They were Russians who had just been laid down next to a stream. They were lapping the water convulsively.

"Nothing could be worse! Fatal if they drink!"

And to my father:

"Your casualty, put him down!"

He examined the Russian closely; seeing him covered in leaves, he realised that he himself was the same and shook himself like a spaniel, still keeping his eyes on the man.

My father laid the body down at his feet.

"Dark blue pupil. Complete contamination. No hope."

The Professor had suddenly assumed the manner of a doctor, and his fingers which had just closed the eye-lid moved over the cheek with a vague, automatic caress.

"Leave him. You'd do better to help us organise!"

Close by, a Russian major, released from his mask, was coming to: his eyes were open, the icy blue of the cornea grew paler, the pupil became clear. Death was leaving him like sleep.

"Try to bring the ambulances up as far forward as possible," Wurtz shouted. "Or at least one. Plenty of casualties on our side as well."

My father could see only Russians. One of them dashed up, embraced him, took a photograph out of his pocket: his wife and children. They would pray for him. He was mistaking the man who had saved him. My father vaguely heard the engines of the ambulances in the gusts of wind, and rushed off in the direction of the sound. Every muscle was now free of the weight of the body, but the shooting pain in his leg made him want to be sick. As the wind died down, the noise of the engines dwindled as though the ambulances were far off, and in every gap in the foliage, in every clear space, my father tried to find a view which would include a glimpse of the road. Coming out of the gas-infected forest, he crossed a wilderness of nettles and dodder, and gazed with wonder on their brilliance, their live green, the fine saw-tooth leaves of the nettles, the white-hot glow of the dodder; so amazed to see colour again that he imagined he saw wherever he looked the small, distant spots of the camouflaged ambulances. Many of the bramble-bushes had already turned the same purple as Virginia creeper; in front of them the incandescent blue of the harebells and the chicory, and the white of the wild carrot, their petals twisted back by the wind, were so intense that he could not help blinking. In the sparkle and flicker of such colouring, the noise of the ambulances which were still out of sight grew louder, faded away into the distance, started up again, and now and then, magnified by an unaccountable echo, seemed to be all round my father.

Finally the noise remained steady, even when the wind fell; the ambulances were coming up not towards my father, but to his left. He rushed off in that direction: the engines he had been hearing were not the ambulances, but some trucks at the head of a column.

As they passed, first the drivers, then the soldiers looked at him in amazement: belt-buckle, hooks, every metal part of his uniform was covered in verdigris. They looked at him with the same uneasiness as men meeting the first native in an unknown land; in the same way they would soon be looking at the first gas casualty. In addition to his pack each man was carrying a fairly large sack at his side: a gas mask. My father also looked at them, one after the other: the barrage of pity would not last indefinitely. Man can get used to anything, except to dying.

"Any ambulances with you?" my father shouted to the first N.C.O.

"Yes. To the rear."

He reached them, issued his orders. They drove up ahead of the column, and my father now felt useless—drained. The tiny blades of the tufted grass, and their flowers, their constellations of leaflets, lay outlined in the white dust at his feet; the nettles, live once more, embedded their wrought-iron stems all over this carpet of humble, quivering reeds. Made of the same brittle straw, insects were scuttling in and out of these slender crops, which alternately quivered with the distant tramp of boots on the road or blew about in the breeze; yellow against his uniform, which was still plastered with leaves, a grass-hopper landed on my father's leg. Just as the gas had shrouded everything in one and the same putrescence, now life seemed to be born again of one single element, of this straw whose hair-spring tension quickened at the same time the lightest tufts of grass and the dainty dart of the grasshopper which had already vanished into the sun-drenched dust. Over the huge curtain of trees the wind was blowing with the same oceanic whistling noise that it makes through poplars.

He was not released, however, from that moment when he had lifted the first dead Russian on to his back. His shoulders still felt the weight of the shifting body; his hands, still trembling, remembered that instant when he had opened them, when that absurd sunflower bracelet had crackled (and the two hedge-hogs in the bottom of the trench, directly below him, two little brooms with bristles fiercely frizzled by the gas—he had scarcely noticed them then). Was it pity? he vaguely wondered, as he had wondered when he had seen the companies retreating; it was something a good deal deeper, an urge in which pain and brotherhood were inseparably united, an urge that came from far back in the past—as though the sheet of gas had yielded not those Russians, but only the friendly bodies of men in the same file. As far as the dazzling blue sky, the hillside sloped upwards with its rediscovered smell of trees, the smell of box-wood and fir trees rustling under a shower of rain. All of a sudden there flashed through his mind the memory of Altenburg: opposite my father were some huge clumps of walnut trees.

A large metal-coloured insect flew off, flashing and burnished—without verdigris. The murmur of the words heard in the dug-out matched its buzzing rather than the oceanic sound of the wind, just as he himself matched the troops disappearing round the corner engaged on wiping out the blinding moment that had carried him away. What was even the earthly adventure behind that window of Reichbach, compared with this human apocalypse that had just seized him by the throat, compared to this spark that had illuminated the depths of the earth that teemed with monsters and buried gods, a chaos like the forest in which stricken and dead swarmed like brothers under the blood-stained greatcoats gesticulating in the wind? A mystery that would not yield its secret but only its presence, a presence so simple and so absolute that it cast into nothingness all thought connected with it—in the same way no doubt as does the presence of death.

Sinking down on to the grass, he lit a cigarette. Foul. Another one: same taste; a third. He threw it away: the bitter-sweet taste persisted. He was already off the road and rushing through the forest with all his strength restored: he was poisoned. It was impossible, it was too late; and it was only his knee that was hurting him . . . In a single second of delirium, the room and the green avenue of Reichbach were mixed up with the droning voice of the Professor under the stars of Bolgako (only yesterday! only yesterday!). But what on earth did man think he was up to? Oh flaming absurdity! Pain stabbed through his leg and into the pit of his stomach each time his right foot touched the ground; he was running, running, and through the whistling of the wind in the branches he could hear quite clearly in his own throat the thin hissing of his breath—a silky sound.

He was no longer even thinking of the fearful faces

that were now in their turn threatening him; in leaps and bounds, every step a knife thrust into his groin, and that merciless taste at the back of his nose and throat, furious at having to slow up on every slope, he was overwhelmed by a lightning-flash of certainty, as urgent as this slight hissing in his throat: the aim of life was happiness, and he, fool that he was, had been engaged on other things instead of being happy! Scruples, human dignity, pity, thought were nothing but a monstrous fake, the bird-calls of a sinister power whose mocking laughter would ring in one's ears in one's last instant of life. In this fierce betrayal and in the clutch of death, there remained only a wild hatred of all that had stopped him being happy. He imagined he saw the ambulance; he tried to run still faster; his legs thrashed the empty air, the whole world suddenly turned upside down, the forest hurtled into a sky which was at the same time under his feet.

He was still semi-conscious. He was being carried. He could make out the sun gleaming on the metalwork of a gas mask, and next to him the gesticulations of a Russian officer: "Don't poison me now, not now!" he was shouting, trying to push the mask away; his cries could not drown the sound of my father's breathing, which was wailing from the pit of his lungs like a fog-horn through the mist, until he lost consciousness completely.

Chartres Camp

THE rest of these "encounters" of my father's— and of his life itself—belong to the same range, but not to the same slope. So I come back to myself: I am in a hurry to get to the point at which writing, at last, is no longer only a change of hell. In this place one is less than oneself; but not less than a man. Now that the chaos of defeat is settled, we are being properly treated. But my investigation, mingling in an undertone with my father's, is every day made more complicated by the destruction of thousands of my friends, in which they seem to acquiesce.

Just as Stieglitz's friend in prison could think only of the three books that "held out" against shame and solitude, so I can think only of what holds out against the spell of nothingness. And from wasted day to wasted day I am increasingly obsessed by the mystery which does not conflict with the indeterminate aspect of my companions who sing while they hold out under the infinity of the night sky. Rather does it link it up, by a long-forgotten path, with the nobility which men do not know exists in themselves, with the victorious side to the only animal that knows he has to die.

A road that is always the same bordered by trees that are always the same, and the stones of Flanders as hard as ever under the tracks of the tanks. The boredom of the convoys on the roads across the plain. Our last boring road; from now on it will be either excitement or fear: we are moving up to the front. Our thoughts burn like a night-light in the deadening heat, the din of the engines and the hammering of the tracks which seem to strike against our heads as much as against the road. I know how our faces look when we get out of the tanks after a long lap, the dull features and fluttering eyes of men who have been bludgeoned, comedians' faces under our lansquenet helmets.

In front of us, the boundless Flemish darkness. Behind us, nine months of barracks and cantonments; the time it takes to make a man.

Nine months ago I was in a hotel in Quercy. The maids never stopped listening to the wireless. They were old women. I passed two of them on the stairs one morning; they were rushing up to their rooms, pitter-pattering up, and tears were streaming down their impassive faces. That was how I found out that the German Army had invaded Poland.

In the afternoon I saw the call-up notices at Beaulieu-sur-Dordogne. Beaulieu church has one of the finest Roman tympana, the only one in which, behind Christ's arms embracing the world, the sculptor has depicted the arms of the cross like a threatening shadow. A tropical downpour had flooded the village. There is a statue of the Virgin Mary in front of the church; as they have done every year for five hundred years to celebrate the wine harvest, the harvesters had fastened one of the best bunches of grapes to the Infant's hand. The peeling notices on the deserted square were beginning to droop; in the presence of the anguish and pity of the unknown sculptor, the raindrops on the bunch tumbled from grape to grape and in the silence fell with scarcely a sound, one after the other, into a puddle.

Our tanks are rolling along in the direction of the German lines. There are four of us in ours. Nothing to do but follow this road in the night and come closer and closer to the war. The life of each one of my friends is now his fate; it may be tonight that they will die.

At the beginning of September I saw them leave in their thousands, anonymous men like my comrades: five million reported to the barracks without a word; it is already a thing of the past, a past which in retrospect is nothing but a great silence.

On the square at Moulins the loudspeaker was announcing the first engagements. Night was falling. Two or three thousand conscripts were listening, ill at ease in their new uniforms because they were new, or in their old ones because they were dirty: not one of them said a word. Along every road the men were reporting for duty, sad-faced women were leading the horses off to be requisitioned. There was a bitter fortitude about all this, the peasant determination in the face of annihilation. They were mounting the scaffold.

191

It is almost in the same spirit that my three companions tonight are rolling along the bleak road in the direction of the German tanks and guns.

Bonneau, the mechanic, should be in the engine-room: I am certain he is in the passage. (In all the tanks which one behind the other are following this road in the night, there is not a single mechanic who has not left the engine-room, where, by order, he should stay.) Since he cannot talk to any of us, he is probably talking to himself, his endless monologue drowned by the hammering of the tracks.

When he came to the squadron under escort, unshaven, in a leather jacket, he looked such a sight that the captain at once put him under the orders of a professional boxer, who at once took delivery of Bonneau in a blue funk. I have seldom noticed real courage in boxing fans.

Anyway, there was no boxing. Only, to begin with, a certain uneasiness. Bonneau had arrived dressed up like a pimp, accustomed to inspire scorn or fear, wishing to inspire more fear the more he met with scorn. But simple soldiers are never scornful, and when Bonneau, thrusting his jaw out, would demand: "What d'you mean by looking at me like that?" the only answer he got was a vague: "Me? I wasn't even looking at you."

He claimed to have killed a man in a brawl, which must have been untrue for he would have been posted to a disciplinary squad. But the orderly room was not slow to let the barracks know that he had been had up three times for assault. The working-class is far less affected than the middle class by the romantic side of murder: to them a murderer is only a particular species, like the wolf. What they had to find out was whether Bonneau really belonged to that species, whether "all that stuff was genuine or just line-shooting". Slaves have a keen scent for lies.

The only one who believed in this fantasy was himself. Prison talk, stories about pimping, statements that "he wanted to let his whiskers grow", so as to be given permission not to shave and so to preserve a good old murderer's face: and the characteristic dead-end way he had of talking, and the Montéhus songs he sang during the cleaning fatigues to which he was more or less permanently condemned. The child of misfortune . . . The whole squadron was crowded together on a staircase, waiting for the issue of boots, when the "Légionnaire" was suddenly heard, then a monologue began: "Ah, what a peach of a girl I once had! I really loved her, that one! Those sods killed her . . ." The picture of a hospital was conjured up, in which "those sods" were at the same time the doctors and all law-abiders, and his cautious mess-mates, although jostling each other like schoolboys confronted with the practical joker, prudently and by devious means saw to it that he was never barrack-room orderly. And they began to learn something about low-life folklore, which in any case was not an entirely closed book to any of them: the victim of society expelled from it through either drink or sex; the rioter of the disciplinary squads; the rebel fighting single-handed against a whole police force in some Fort Chabrol; the Bonnot (and ours certainly did not forget that his name was almost identical) firing on the inspector right through his own forearm; but above all the brave, sentimental pimp, a dirty dog but steady, faithful to his friends and murdering for love, who, having escaped from the chain-gang, has his saturnine existence cut short by the alligators of the Maroni. For, whether his "sods" are heroes or wretches, Bonneau's hell is only a circle, and that is a circle of victims.

When he brought in an injured chaffinch and said he was going to keep it, fear of him increased: in the eyes of these friends of mine, the murderer is first and foremost a madman.

The more strictly the lighting system was controlled, the more ingenious was the camouflage in each barrack-room. The N.C.O.s would take out the bulbs but, when the time came, other bulbs would pop up from under the bolsters. One night two switches would not work. Bonneau claimed "he knew about electricity", struggled secretly with all the fuse-boxes in the whole building, and did so well that that night there was not a single switch working in his own barrack-room or in four others. Growls could be heard in the darkness: "Who the devil saddled us with a chap like that!" "Just our luck to be landed with such a pipsqueak!" "Well, I'm an electrician, but I wouldn't meddle unless they told me to, and now this fellow!" From the way the door of the first barrack-room was slammed, everyone realised it was he coming in; silence fell at once. Then a vague squabble started, and a voice, quite cool, precise and hard, and not the boxing corporal's voice: "Look here, Bonneau, we're getting a bit fed up with you. I don't give a damn for tough guys. If they're going to bugger up my bulb, bad luck on them. And if you don't like it, take a look at me." (A face loomed up, brightly lit by the small circle of a torch.) "If you want to look for me tomorrow, it won't be hard to find me!"

That was the first time I heard Pradé speaking.

And Bonneau began to explain in the dark "that it wasn't his fault, that the current . . . that the fuses . . ." I was expecting everyone to say that he was frightened: the general impression was that "he wasn't really climbing down so much, that he was a steady chap, that he didn't argue when he knew he was in the wrong . . ." So he was not so crazy. The squadron was almost ready to adopt him, but the barrack-room remained without a light.

A tank-driver, an ex-bus-driver, started singing "Le P'tit Quinquin". There were quite a number of soldiers from Flanders there, but it was not nostalgia that gave such force to his singing, it was his slow tempo. He made a funereal chant of it, and in the same way that he was following the true dirge-like rhythm, he followed the nasal manner of singing, as though it only needed a melancholy voice in this darkness to give a song of sadness its full meaning. And the soldiers asked for it again, verse after verse, just as they would ask for glass after glass in the canteen, bent on getting drunk in this war which to them was like a prison.

Tired of this music that was lacking in glory, the singer began the grand aria from Tosca. Catastrophically. An embarrassed silence followed the last howls; the driver angrily mumbled: "All right then, if these gentlemen don't like it," went back to bed, and to the mournfulness of the first song was added the uneasy feeling that a common bond between them had been destroyed. Bonneau was forgotten. Everyone sank into his own individual depression. Which of them was the first to take the photograph of his wife out of his wallet, to look at it by the secret gleam of a torch? Five minutes later, pictures were being passed around among the small groups, four or five taws round a dim light, amateur snapshots falling on to the straw from clumsy fingers amid cries of abuse. In any case not one of them gave a damn for the others' wives, but only looked at them in order to be able to show his own. And yet, in this intimate light, they looked like secrets, the women's clothes suddenly giving a better idea of their husbands' lives than the men's photographs in civilian clothes would have done. Pradé's was a housewife carved out of hard wood with flat ribbons in her hair; Bonneau was the only one of us to own four photographs, each more whorish than the last. And little beetroot-nosed Léonard —our wireless-operator—shy and having to be asked twice, finally took out a postcard, a gorgeous girl in a dazzling feathered dress. There were a few words written at the foot of it. And with their heads glued to each other under Léonard's nose, which was lit fantastically from underneath, the mess-mates could see, as they bent over the torch: "To darling little Louis" and the signature of one of the stars of the music-halls.

Léonard had been a fireman at the Casino de Paris.

Every night with unabated admiration he used to watch the star coming off, glowing from the applause. He claims he never spoke to her. His face can be attractive in spite of his extraordinary schnozzle: soft spaniel eyes and, what is occasionally pathetic, an expression completely devoid of conceit. Was the dancer touched by his undying admiration; was it a whim on her part? One exceptionally successful night "when the applause could still be heard even as she was going upstairs", she took him into her dressing-room and slept with him. "But the funny part of it all is—well, when we were in bed, she suddenly sees my uniform on the chair and then, as if she was going to jump out of her skin, she says: 'Here, you're not in the police, are you?' 'Of course not, can't you see it's the fire-brigade!' 'Because if you were . . .' Funny, eh? She used to see me every evening and she didn't know the fire-brigade. Must admit, though, in those days I was younger . . ."

Each of them has his own dream, Marlene Dietrich, or Mistinguett, or the Duchess of Windsor, but it remains a dream. And they do not look on this pal of theirs to whom the goddesses have spoken—this madcap of the mess—merely as a lucky chap, but as a man of destiny; to them his little frizzled head with its red nose is proof of the mysterious side of love, and, although they do not know it, what intrigues them about the actress's whim is the love-potion of Isolde.

"Well, what happened afterwards?" they asked in chorus, and their fingers trembled as they handled the photograph again.

"The next few days she didn't make a sign, so I realised . . ."

He spoke without bitterness, even without resignation; he was in agreement.

Their inheritance has not made them free-and-easy in the face of happiness.

It goes without saying that the most popular, after Léonard's photograph, were the four photographs belonging to Bonneau. The latter was certainly being taken up by the squadron. And gradually, at the sight of him stooping down during a route march to pick up an old knife, putting it in his cartridge-pouch with a fresh statement of opinion: "They're no good, these tools!" invariably ending up with: "It may come in handy!" they realised that this figure of terror only concealed a rag-and-bone man, and everyone knows what a rag-and-bone man is like. Then the passage of time made this anarchist reveal yet another side to his nature: a respect for priests: "My ma didn't teach me much, but she did teach me to respect those people! Why did the State take everything they had away from them? Robbery, that's what I call it. It's the Rothschilds, the bankers, chaps like that who did it; it's always the poor that are robbed!" He stood up for the Ruhr Occupation Medal, worshipped Captain de Mortemart "who was with me in the Hussars, at Strasbourg, not like the fatheads here, he knew how to command, could take off his pips and tell a chap: 'If you're a man, come outside!' " He was always ready, if he were a corporal, to think of himself as a model soldier, good-hearted and muddle-headed, without, however, denying Montéhus. A member of the benevolent society, and a respecter of respectability. "Come now, Bonneau," said the lieutenant, "you're not as bad as you would like to make out!" "Me sir? But I'm not a bad chap! It's the others who've made me bad." His thick lips are pursed, his black eyebrows are raised, and the removal of his mask of "terror", seems suddenly to reveal his incurably childish soul.

He did not hold it against Pradé for what he had said. We are the crew of a tank, and often go to the canteen together; as soon as Bonneau starts shooting a line, Pradé shrugs his shoulders slightly and looks at him without saying a word. Bonneau splutters, and feels he is face to face with a different species—one that never dreams.

That was how we were, sitting round a litre of red wine after leaving the lecture which we had attended, in column of fours, to be told the necessity for dismembering Germany. I was anxious to know what the soldiers thought of that noble talk, as a result of which dinner had been postponed for an hour.

"Better if they'd let us eat at the proper time," said Bonneau.

And Léonard:

"Well, I like to listen to educated chaps . . ."

And others round us:

"I didn't quite get it; he talked like a book."

"What the hell; all we want is to get back home."

Yet another:

"Fine words to make us commit beastly deeds!"

"What kind?"

A vague gesture.

But they were all faintly aware that when it came to dismembering Germany they would not be asked for their opinion; and that when the high-ups wanted to convince them of no matter what, it was best to be on their guard. Closed up within himself like an Oriental (and he had the flat face and slanting eyes of an Oriental himself), Pradé once again had said nothing.

We came back to the barrack-room together, by ourselves. We had gone a good hundred yards without uttering a word, when he made up his mind and, without looking at me at first, said in his heavy east-country accent and slow delivery:

"It's about what you've just asked the chaps: what they think about that smart-alec's speech. Pradé thinks that it's one thing to talk to soldiers, and quite another to talk to French citizens. As a soldier I'm prepared to listen to anything; I shan't hear any more than I've already had to hear! But if they talk to me as a citizen, then it's not the same thing. It's not the same!" Whenever he talks, he seems to be answering some invisible liar. "In that case I don't like to be forced to think. Nor to listen to a lot of balls. I know the Jerries, I know them, I do. When they arrived at our place in '15, they found everyone in the cellars. They beat on the doors with their rifle-butts: I was a kid, so I was sent to open up. I used to tremble like this. There were some who boxed our ears for us, there were others who gave us bread. Just like anywhere else."

He repeated these words, his toothless jaws thrust out, still angry with the imaginary liar:

"Just like anywhere else."

And he added in the same tone:

"But they don't bother to talk about citizens!"

It often seems that these soldiers with whom I am living are men of another period in history. Listening to Pradé, I imagined I heard the old republican dignity, a voice that has scarcely changed for a hundred years. He had taken me into his confidence, told me that one of his brothers, a hot-head, had come back from the International Brigade. "And when you come back from that, it's Pradé telling you, no use trying to look for a job!" But one day he came up to me and, in his usual slow voice, in his accent that seemed to stress everything with his fist, to make each sentence an abrupt summing-up of his thoughts: "The captain's batman's in a bad way. In the army, a batman's not such a bad job . . ." I waited. Whenever he comes up to me like this, starting off with a general statement, it is to ask for my assistance and advice. He went on:

"There's nothing worse than an officer . . ."

"Then why put yourself into his hands, and in the position of a servant?"

"A servant?" (and once again bitterly thrusting out his stumps) "who isn't a servant here? But I say that when you're a batman, you deal less with the chump himself than with his old woman. A steady man who does his job, I say, who does his job," (and that gesture he so often uses, meaning: "I'm serving you, and leave

it at that; slave or not, I have the right not to know you")
"that man manages to get some peace. With an officer,
and everyone else there is between him and us, you
never get any peace. A woman's only a woman; but at
least she doesn't wear pips!"

I did not dare use the word "dignity"; I went about it
in a roundabout way; but he used it at once:

"If a man has any dignity, he's got it whatever the
circumstances; if not, then I say he hasn't any at all!"

And as I tried to explain to him that human relationship in the army was at least an impersonal one, he smiled
bitterly, showing his stumps of teeth; and I felt that he
was right, that he was capable of living for ten years next
to a man whom he did not care for, and could see him
die, as though that man had never existed.

His son is all that stands for the absolute in this
degrading, gloomy, troublesome adventure called life.
When he asks me if I think the war will last long, it is
not because he wants to know how long he will be in
the army:

"The lad's eleven; that's a little older than I was in the
last war. That's what stopped me getting an education.
They managed to send me to Sunday school, all right,
but they couldn't send me to college. He's bright, the
kid, he's a bright one. I could have got him a scholarship.
But what's happened to all the scholarships with this
war on? For him to go on with his studies, I'd have to
work, and the only work I'm doing is playing around
with rifles. And afterwards, if he misses two years, there'll
be nothing we can do, it'll be too late. He's the first one

in my family who could have had a proper education. At that age, no matter how, a kid has got to be helped. I could still help him. Beyond school certificate I couldn't, but at this stage I still could, except for spelling. I've tackled sums on purpose. I could help him. But what can my wife do?

"She comes from a very large family . . ."

And, in that tone of considered opinion which he often uses, sad now instead of angry:

"She's not very bright."

It is he who is driving. And since the intercommunication on our tanks, although they are fairly new, does not work between the tank-commander and the driver, we are connected by two strings fastened to his arms, which I hold in my hands.

In spite of the din of the tracks we suddenly seem to be plunged into silence; the tanks have just moved off the road. Like a canoe released from a sandbank, like an aeroplane taking off, we enter our true element; our muscles which have been tensed against the vibration of the armour-plating, against the ceaseless hammering of the tracks on the road, now relax, yielding to the peace of the moonlight.

For a minute we roll along, released like this, between the stunted, flowering orchards and the long banks of mist. In the smell of castor oil and burnt rubber I nervously hold my strings, ready to stop the tank in order to fire: the surface even of these apparently smooth fields is too uneven for the tank to be trimmed while it is still running. Since we have left the road, and the occasional shapes we can now make out might be targets, we are all the more conscious of the way we are pitching like a sharp-prowed galleon. Clouds conceal the moon. We are entering the cornfields.

This is the moment the war begins.

There is no word to describe what one feels when advancing on the enemy, and yet it is just as specific, just as powerful as sexual desire or pain. The whole world becomes an insensible menace. We are steering by compass and can see only what is outlined against the sky; telegraph-poles, roofs, tree-tops, the orchards which are only a little more distinct than the mist have disappeared, the shadows seem to be massed at the level of the fields which rock us or furiously shake us; if a track breaks, we are either dead or prisoners. I can tell how closely Pradé's slanting eyes are watching his dashboard, I can feel the string tickling my hand every second, as though a bump was going to warn me. And we are not yet in contact. The war awaits us a little further on, perhaps behind the folds of ground bristling here and there with telegraph-poles, their concrete phosphorescent in the light of the moon which has come out again.

The long, shadowy lines of the plain in the night, the banks of mist coming up again all white, rise and fall with every lurch of the tank. Against the sudden, harsh bumps, against the frenzied vibrations whenever we hit a patch of hard ground in the cornfields, the whole of our body is hunched, like a motor-car at the moment of a collision. I am clinging on to the turret not so much with my hands as with my back muscles. If the violent vibrations crack one of the petrol feeds, the tank will meet the shell by turning over on itself like an epileptic cat. But the tracks are still hammering the fields and the stones, and, through the slits in the turret, beyond what I can see of the short corn, the mist and the orchards, I watch the horizon still unstreaked by any gun flash rising and falling in the night sky.

The German positions are in front of us; the only places where our tanks can be effectively hit head-on are the look-out slit and the gun-shield. We have faith in our armour. The enemy is not the German, it is the track breaking, the mine and the anti-tank ditch.

Our main obsession is the ditch. One does not talk about the mine any more than one talks about death; one either blows up or one does not, it is not a subject of conversation. The ditch is: we have heard accounts of the last war—and while training we saw the modern ditches, with slanting bottoms to prevent the tank from lifting its nose, and with four anti-tank guns automatically set off by the fall of the tank. Léonard, Bonneau, Pradé, there is not one of us who has not imagined himself caught between four intersecting anti-tank guns at the moment they are about to fire. And the world of ditches is a vast one, ranging from this complete destruction to the hastily camouflaged hole where the fall only sets off a signal to a heavy gun trained in the distance, and to the simple pit. Nothing remains of the old fellow-feeling between man and earth: these corn-fields through which we are pitching in the night are no longer cornfields but camouflage; there are no fields for harvesting, there are only fields of ditches, fields of mines; and it seems that the tank is creeping of its own accord into some ambush constructed by itself, that the human species of the future are tonight embarking on the real battle, which is something beyond the human adventure.

On a low hill some purple flashes presently appear in quick succession: the heavy German artillery. Was this sudden blaze invisible in the moonlight or has the barrage just begun? It stretches, as far as our pitching turrets let us see, mainly from right to left, as though a huge match was being scratched along the whole horizon. But no explosion near us. Our engines drown every other noise; we have probably left the cornfields (I cannot see further than twenty yards), for the angry clang of the tracks starts hammering us again. I call a halt for a second.

In the silence eating into me comes the gun-fire, thudding away on the wind. And while our own clattering still faintly echoes in my ear, through the burst of some shells behind us and the sudden hammering of our unit's tracks, the same wind brings the deep noise of the forest, the rustling of great curtains of poplars: the invisible French tanks advancing into the depths of the night.

The firing stops. Behind us, then in front, an occasional shell still bursts; and as the crimson flash vanishes, an expectant silence ensues, full of the rattle of our tanks.

We move off again, forcing the pace so as to catch up with our invisible group. The hammering of the tracks has started again and once again we go deaf, Pradé and I glued once more to the armour-plating and the hand-grips, eyes painfully peering out for a gush of stones and earth followed by a fiery explosion which we shall never hear. Towards the German lines the wind is blowing pools of stars in confusion between the huge clouds.

Nothing seems slower than moving into action. In the May mist the two other tanks in our group are advancing on our left; further off, the other groups; still further, and to the rear, all the sections are moving into position in the moonlight. I am sure that Léonard and Bonneau, who are blind against the armour-plating, are aware of it as much as Pradé who is glued to his periscope, as much as myself who am glued to my slits; I can feel it in my bones as much as I can feel the grip of the tracks on the slippery earth—the parallel thrust of the tanks through the night. Opposite us, other tanks are advancing against us through the same clear night: men equally tense, equally absorbed. But who, for the last seven years, have been preparing for war. The noses of our tanks on the left are rising and falling against the clearer background of the cornfields. Behind them, shock troops in light tanks are moving up; and further off the deep masses of the French infantry. The peasants whom I saw silently marching off to the army on every road in France at the beginning of September are now converging on the sinister stream of our squadron across the Flemish plain. Oh, may victory rest with those who went to war without liking it!

Is this excitement that is eating into me due to my part in an action involving bloodshed, is it due to the disturbing, solemn quality inherent in human sacrifice? How I pray that none of these men will die! In the moonlight our tracks are shimmering through the young corn.

Suddenly every shape close to us disappears, except for the tree-tops; there is nothing at ground level; darkness spreads over the tanks that are with us. No doubt a cloud is masking the moon which is now too high in the sky for me to be able to see it through the slits. And once again we think of the mine towards which we are being driven through the yielding cornfields by the revolutions of the oiled cogwheels; and the friendly shadows round us vanish. Cut off from everything that is not Pradé, Léonard, Bonneau, Berger: a single crew— on its own.

Léonard's hand appears between my thighs and the turret, puts a piece of paper down beside the compass. I light up and my eyes, suddenly blinded by the glare, eventually decipher the letters through the scarlet suns: "Tank B.21 up against ditch."

Pradé switches off. Through the gaps in the clouds the clear moonlight sweeps the ground again and again. Now our tanks are falling back a little; we have passed them. Then, a hundred yards ahead, a dramatic burst of shells right on to our vibrating armour. The smoke, which for a second looked red, curls in the wind, strangely black and opaque in the moonlight.

More explosions. Not many. It is not even curtain

fire. The whole squadron is now moving more quickly, but not yet at full speed. What is the meaning of this sporadic bombardment? Are the Germans short of artillery? I switch my gaze to my dimly luminous compass, which quivers, swerves, swings back, seems anxious to veer off the course but, with every heave on the steering-wheel, swings back again, like our life pointlessly and ceaselessly fighting against our fate. From time to time I pull one of the strings, correct Pradé's steering; the tank begins to skid along the surface which is now hard and uneven. Suddenly we are sliding in panic on a surface which is giving way.

It is not true that one sees the whole of one's past life on the point of death!

Above me, someone is yelling. Bonneau? Léonard has his arms wrapped round my legs and is shouting: "Pradé! Pradé!" I can hear him through my thighs, and his yells are as feeble and shrill as the cries of a bird in the cataclysmic silence that has fallen since Pradé, on feeling the thud, jammed on the brakes.

The ditch.

I too am yelling. The engine starting up drowns every voice.

Pradé pushes the slanting tank forward.

"Back! Back!"

I pull with all my strength on the right-hand string: it is broken. The shells which were only falling intermittently are the ones that have blown up the pin-pointed ditches. The earth is shaking from the noise of the free tanks passing all around us.

Pradé was only getting a run-up, and is now reversing. How many seconds before the shell? All of us have our heads tucked into our shoulders as far as they will go, and Bonneau is still yelling. Leaning heavily on its nose, its tail in the air like a Japanese fish, the tank backs out, buries itself at an angle in the face of the ditch, vibrating from end to end, like a thrown hatchet quivering in a tree-trunk. It slips, collapses. Is it blood or sweat running down my nose? We have fallen sideways on. Bonneau, still yelling, tries to open the side door, cannot manage and shuts it again. It can now only be opened from underneath. One of the tracks is thrashing the empty air; Pradé heaves the tank on to the other one, and it falls like a log, as though crashing into a second ditch. My helmet bangs against the turret, and my head seems to be swelling, swelling, although anticipation of the shell is still driving it into my shoulders like a screw. If the bottom of the ditch is soft, then we are sunk, and the shell can take its time. No, the tank is moving forward, backing, starting off again. The bottom of modern ditches wedges a tank in, and the intersecting anti-tank guns should have fired already; this must be a pin-pointed ditch. The back face is unassailable; if the front face is vertical or slanting, maybe we shall get out (but before the shell); if we are in a funnel, we shall never get out, never get out, never get out. I try to see until it hurts my eyes; beads of moisture slide over my forehead, my eye-sockets are cold with sweat. The invisible face must be quite close. In his terror Bonneau keeps opening and shutting the door with all his strength, and in spite of the din of the engine in the ditch the armour-plating rings like a bell. Why has the shell not come? Léonard has let go of my legs and is pulverising them with kicks. He wants to open the door of my turret. The shell will burst in the ditch, one cannot get out of a ditch, to rush out of the tank would be even more stupid than to stay paralysed inside it, between a madman trying to break one's legs and another, crazily frightened of getting out, frightened of staying inside, beating the sinister tom-toms of madness by slamming the door. I am not calm like a man who is calm; I am beyond hysteria. I leave the turret, bend down to get to Pradé, who suddenly switches on the lights. The shell will not come; they don't kill you in broad daylight, they only kill you in the dark.

While I have been bending down to get into the passage of the tank, Léonard has slipped into the turret in my place; at last he opens the door in it, stands there gaping; he does not jump out, but crouches suddenly and turns to me without saying a word, his drunkard's nose extraordinarily red in the raw moonlight; terror makes him keep his head still but his shoulders are shaking against the black background of the door opened on to the ditch. The tracks are not gripping. We are in a funnel. On hands and knees I push forward towards Pradé, send Bonneau flying; he is still yelling and tugging at the side door. I shout down the passage:

"Cut it out!"

"Me? I didn't say anything!" he replies in a suddenly normal voice which I can hear in spite of the din of the engine; he is looking me straight in the eye; quaking like a child who expects a slap in the face; he gets up, banging his helmet right into the roof of the tank, falls back on to his knees. His theatrical, terrified face has assumed a horribly innocent expression in the presence of death.

"I didn't say anything," he repeats (at the same time he is listening, like me, like all of us, waiting for the shell); letting go of the door, he stares into my eyes, and with arms outstretched, with his helmet forced over his eyes by the crash like a saucepan-lid, lurching with the jolt of the skidding tracks, he yells, yells, without taking his eyes off me.

I get up to Pradé, am able to stand upright for a bit. We are right in the front of the tank, the nose of which is in the air, and gradually my dangling body is raised up, as though this tank illuminated in the ditch was offering me as a sacrifice to death. Are we going to fall back in again? I am wedged firm at last. Our tracks are still slipping: my oily hands covered with blood claw the air like an animal burrowing, as though I was myself a tank.

The tracks are gripping!

A camouflaged "elephant pit"? In a ditch the tracks would not grip. Shall we be able to get out before the shell? The three men with me have become my oldest friends. Like an explosion, a door bangs again! Perhaps the German gunners have not seen the signal of the tank's crash because of a fold in the ground, perhaps the look-out is nodding, perhaps . . . What nonsense! But it is greater nonsense to hope that there are ditches without guns trained on them! The tracks are still gripping.

Pradé switches off.

"What the hell are you up to?"

In spite of my longing to get out, I can feel the silence growing round us like a breastplate; so long as we hear nothing whistling overhead, we are alive for four seconds. When will that door stop banging? I am listening with the same mad concentration with which I have up to now been looking, and through the gong-beat of the door I can only hear the thunder of our waves of tanks reverberating from the ditch and from our armour, passing us and disappearing. With my helmet glued to Pradé's, I yell into the hole of his ear-pieces: "Get her up!" my voice filling the tank in the strange new silence. With his legs in the air, wedged against the motionless, rearing tank by his seat, Pradé turns to me; like Bonneau's face, his old face, in spite of the helmet, has grown innocent; his eyes staring stupidly, his three teeth sketching a smile like the patient smile of a dying man:

"This time the lad's had it for sure . . . The tracks are beginning to slip again."

He is almost whispering. Through his words I try to listen for the indistinct, incipient whistle of a shell:

"If we go on like this, we'll get bogged down on our belly."

The whistle . . . Our necks disappear into our shoulders. Pradé has lifted his legs from the pedals in the attitude of a frog, to protect his stomach. The shell bursts thirty yards behind us.

213

The flare has died down. Curled up, we wait for the next shell—not the explosion nor the whistle, but the distant firing-sound—the very voice of death. And suddenly Pradé's oriental face looms up dimly out of the darkness, becomes distinct with the leaden solemnity of the faces of the dead: a mysterious gleam, dim and feeble, fills the tank. And with it, a terror that dislocates my madman's calm: death is warning us. Pradé's motionless face looms further and further out of the shadows, strangely disembodied, divorced by fear from every vestige of life. I am no longer even listening: the shell is bound to come, for death is already lurking in the tank. Turning his face to me, Pradé catches sight of me, and from his hunched neck, which is released from the tension of the shell by a supernatural terror, he jerks his head backwards straight into the armour-plating. And the bang of the helmet like a bell in the silence dispels the terrifying presence, allows me to get to the viewfinder of the periscope at last: the rearing tank is looking up at the sky in which the moon has just come out, and what is now lighting up our faces, which are drained of life, is the mirror reflecting this moon-filled sky, vast and teeming once more with stars.

Our deliverance lies in ridding ourselves of the suspense of the shell. The door is still banging. A hand has seized my back and is nudging it. I should like to shake it off, but I am hanging in mid-air.

"We can get out, you chaps! We can get out!" Léonard's childish voice is shouting. It is he who is shaking my back. He has got out of the tank during our manoeuvring. He clambers into the passage, which is now vertical, studded with instruments, as though he was mounting a scaffold.

"There's some rubble here! It's a sort of ditch! At least twenty yards long, maybe thirty! With rubble in it!"

Pradé at once backs the tank. Léonard and I roll over, thrown flat on to the ground. The tank is horizontal again. I get up, jump through the side door which Léonard has left open, tumble again into a heavy smell of clay, while the tank, still backing, comes to a stop on my left, with only the geometrical shape of the open door illuminated in the darkness in which tank and ditch merge into each other. Pradé has been able to light up again.

Up there, on the surface, our armoured division is still moving forward, making less noise than when we heard them from inside our armour-plating. The shells seem to start slowly, then accelerate in order to reach us. As they start whistling, the sound seems to be aimed at us, directed towards our ditch. Guns are not always trained on the camouflaged traps. But there is no rubble. Léonard is raving, we have fallen into a collapsed funnel. No, the camouflage of the ditch has been pierced in the middle by the tank; every scrap of darkness that is not exactly under this great gap full of stars seems to be converging on it. I go forward. I test the ground; a little further on, the face which we tackled begins to slant. Oh for us not to be killed before we can get out! I dare not switch on my torch. In any case I have left it behind in the tank.

"We can have a try," says Pradé quite close to me in the darkness.

He too is glued to the face of the wall; outside our armour-plating we feel naked. From the clay wall oozes the smell of mushrooms, memories of childhood. Pradé lights a match; it only shows up two yards. Another whistle hurtles towards us, rising then falling as it approaches; with our shoulders pressed into the clay, spellbound by the gap of sky which will be replaced by a flaming red fire, we wait once more. One can never get used to dying. The match stays amazingly still, and its flame flickers. How vulnerable and fragile a human body is! We are flattened against the face of the ditch we share: Berger, Léonard, Bonneau, Pradé—a single cross. Our patch of sky disappears, goes out; clods of earth tumble down on our helmets and shoulders.

Perhaps the Germans have not had time to pin-point the camouflaged traps exactly, and their pounding is guesswork. The shells are grouped.

The waves of tanks are still moving on up there, but in the opposite direction. Has the petrol point been set up here, or are they in retreat? Are we to get out of here only to fall on to the German armoured columns? I am already beginning to believe that we shall get out.

Bonneau's torch flashes on. He is no longer yelling. We move forward, the four of us, still clinging to the clay. I am calm again, but there is a corner of my mind which is still obsessed, which will go on being obsessed, by the thought of the shell. The camouflage stretches in every direction beyond the hole made by the tank as it fell; now the caved-in face rises in an almost gradual slope. We clamber up until we bump into the trunks covering the ditch.

We shall never get to the hole; it is as if we were in one of those dungeons where daylight only comes in through an inaccessible trap-door; the prisoners cannot escape through the roof. The two nearest trunks will have to be pushed aside. Bending over them, whispering: "One, two, three," we test them with our shoulders, petrified like Peruvian mummies at every explosion, but recovering immediately afterwards; since we have been able to take some sort of action, action has taken the place of fear. If we cannot manage the trunks, perhaps the tank will be able to break them up. It is standing behind us, darker than the ditch in the silence; from its half open door comes a beam of light in which some nocturnal insect is flying about.

We race towards it without taking cover, we look on it now as a fortress. Pradé manoeuvres into position in front of the landslide. Loose earth has gathered round it. Up there, the waves are still rolling towards the French lines. We are beginning to get entombed. Pradé places the underditching beam under the tracks; the tank rears, wavers; the tracks grip like hands. The tank climbs further up, jams, races again, stuck fast, wedged against the ceiling of trunks. If these won't give, our efforts will jam us further and further in; before two minutes are out, the body of the tank will be glued to the ground and the tracks will turn in a void.

This time the beam cannot be used.

217

"Let's get some stones!"

Pradé does not answer.

With engines racing, the mass of steel breaks into the trunks, all the armour-plating tightens; with the furious recovery of an angry bull, the tank hurls me like a stone against the turret, in a resounding din of trunks pouring down on to the armour; there is a shout behind me, a helmet clanks, and now we are gliding off like a boat. Getting to my feet, with a single blow I push away Pradé's head, which is glued to the periscope; I switch off; in the mirror, stretching into the distance, the open plain . . .

We are moving forward at full speed between the shell-bursts, each man shrivelled at his post, thinking only of the next ditch. We must not let another tank fall in after us. I am vaguely aware that I should have gone round the ditch and stopped in front of it, or else have waited for our petrol supplies so as to warn the command (but we have to push on), or else have lighted a fire (but with what?). And we must not stay here, we must push on. Stopping means escaping the ditches, but just now nothing counts in face of the orders we have been given, neither the short waves of tanks rolling back, nor the risk being run by those following us, nor the risk we are running ourselves: so we push on. The army. It is not courage, it is automatic reflex. And yet the darkness, which is no longer the tomb of the ditch, the living darkness appears to me like a prodigious gift, a huge germination.

By the time we reach the village the Germans have evacuated it. We go in. Chaos everywhere. We are moving with a strange, loping motion that I am beginning to recognise, the movement of utter weariness, when soldiers march with their heads thrust forward and their mouths hanging open, and can no longer see quite clearly. Since our tank is badly camouflaged (like all the others) we slide down into the straw in a barn. In the beam of my torch, which I have switched on for a second, I can see Pradé lying down, grasping the straw and clutching it as though it was life.

"So it wasn't on our ticket this time," I said.

Perhaps he is thinking that the lad has got out of it.

"The war isn't over yet," he answers with an everlasting smile of bitterness. He lets go of the grass and closes his eyes.

Perhaps we shall be alive again tomorrow.

The morning is as fine as if war did not exist. Day has broken. Pradé woke me when he got up; of all of us he has always been the first to get up:

"Time enough to stay in bed when I'm dead!"

I go off to look for a pump. The cold water not only wakes us from the night's sleep, but also from the thought of the ditch. A few yards away, Pradé sits looking straight in front of him, smiling bitterly through his three stumps and shaking his head:

"If any one had told me that one day I might look at some hens and not find it perfectly natural, I shouldn't have believed it."

And everything that I look at this morning, I also see through the eyes of a stranger. The hens which have not

yet been stolen are wandering about, apparently unaware
of the war, but their small, round eyes follow us with cautious cunning; nearby, some of them are pecking in front
of a barn in which soldiers are asleep. These are the ones
that Pradé is looking at; I also look at this mechanical pecking, the neat thrust of the head released by a spring, and the
warmth of them seems to permeate my hands, as though
I was holding them, the warmth of newlaid eggs—the
warmth of life; the animals are alive on this strange earth.
We walk through a morning devoid of peasants. Muscovy
ducks, magpies—and mosquitoes. In front of us are some
watering-cans with mushroom-shaped spouts, the kind I
used to love as a boy; and it suddenly strikes me that man
has emerged out of the depths of the past simply to invent
a watering-can. On the other side of the hens strutting
coolly or furtively in their freedom, a Siberian rabbit with
heavy hindquarters is trying to jump like a cony; grind-
stones lie gleaming in the sun, spiders' webs hang sparkling with dew; in a daze and for a long time I stare at a
ridiculous flower, born of humanity just as the disordered
mass of flowers round it are born of the earth: a broom . . .
At the swift, supple flight of a cat, I find myself surprised
that this twisting fur really exists. (Besides, all the cats
are in flight. Only the mongrels stay on, as they have
stayed perhaps ever since the arrival of our tanks.) What
is it in me that makes me amazed—my only feeling since
waking has been one of surprise—that on this well-
planned earth the dogs are still behaving like dogs, the
cats like cats? Some grey doves fly off, leaving the tom-cat
under them clutching at the end of its fruitless pounce;

they describe a silent arc in the navy-blue sky, cut it short and, suddenly white, fly off in another direction. I am prepared to see them return and run after the cat which will then take to the air. Those days when animals could talk, the ambiguous poetry of the oldest tales, they come back to one from the other side of one's life . . .

Like a man confronted for the first time with India, I can hear in this picturesque profusion the hum of the centuries buried almost as deep as last night's darkness: these barns bursting with grain and straw, these barns with their beams hidden by husks, full of harrows, canes, poles, wooden carts; barns which consist only of grain, wood, straw and leather (everything in metal has been requisitioned), surrounded by the dead fires of refugees and soldiers, these are the barns of the Gothic Age; our tanks at the end of the road are filling up with water, monsters kneeling at the wells of the Bible. O life, how old you are!

And how stubborn! In every farmyard wood has been gathered for the winter. Our soldiers who are beginning to get up make their first fires from it. Well-planned vegetable-plots everywhere . . . There is nothing here that does not bear man's imprint. In the wind some wooden clothes-pegs are fluttering on the lines like swallows. Some of the clothes hanging up are not yet dry; flimsy stockings, working gloves, farmers' and labourers' over-alls; in this desert of destruction the linen has initials embroidered on it . . .

All we are worth, ourselves and the men opposite, is our mechanics, our courage and our cowardice; but the old race of men which we have chased away and which has only left behind its tools, its washing and its initials on the linen, seems to have risen, across the millennia, from the darkness we were in last night—slowly, greedily laden with all the scrap it has abandoned to us, the barrows and harrows, the biblical carts, the kennels and hutches, the empty ovens.

My legs can still feel Léonard's arms around them; his yells through the hammering of the tank are still buzzing in my ears like flies. Shall I remember forever that childish expression which I had never seen before on Pradé's face, that amazed face of Bonneau's as he stopped yelling to say: "Me? I'm not yelling!" But these ghosts in front of the barns, in the sunlight shimmering on the tips of the young branches, are only there to add to their brilliance.

Once again Pascal comes to my mind: "Imagine a large number of men in chains, and all condemned to death, every day some of them being butchered before the others' eyes, the remainder realising their own plight from the plight of their fellows . . . This is the picture of man's estate." How firmly a meditation of this kind can make men cling to their wretched share of happiness. I remember my father. Perhaps pain is always the more powerful; perhaps the joy granted to the only animal that knows it is not eternal was poisoned from the very start. But this morning I am all birth. I can still feel within me the invasion of the earthly darkness when we came out of the ditch, that germination in shadows deepened by the constellations in the gaps of the drifting clouds; and just as I saw the thundering, teeming night rise up out of the ditch, so now from that night there rises the miraculous revelation of day.

The world might have been as simple as the sky or the sea. And at the sight of these shapes in front of me, which are only the shapes of an abandoned, condemned village; at the sight of these barns of Paradise and the clothes-pegs, these dead fires and wells, these sparse briars and voracious brambles which in a year perhaps will have covered everything over; these animals, these trees, these houses, I feel myself in the presence of an unaccountable gift—an apparition. All this might never have been, might never have been as it is. How these individual shapes harmonise with the earth! There are other worlds, the world of crystals, of oceanic depths. . . . With its trees branching out like veins, the universe is as complete and mysterious as a young body. The door of the farm I am walking past has been left open by the farmers in their flight; I can see a semi-looted room inside. Ah, the three Magi did not bring gifts to the Infant, they only told him that on the night he was born open doors were banging in the dim light—doors opened on to this life which, this morning for the first time, has shown itself as powerful as the darkness and as powerful as death.

Two old peasants are sitting on a bench; the man's jacket is still smeared with the cobwebs from his cellar. Pradé goes up to them with a smile from his three jutting teeth:

"Taking the sun, granpa?"

By his accent the old man has recognised him as a peasant like himself; he looks at him with a dreamy affection, as though he was at the same time looking further into the distance. His wife's hair hangs down in a sorry little grey knot, tightly-plaited. It is she who replies:

"What else can we do? You, you're young; when you're old, there's nothing left but wear and tear . . ."

Propped against the cosmos like a stone . . . Yet she smiles, a slow, pensive, delayed smile; beyond the football-pitch with its solitary goalposts, beyond the tank-turrets gleaming with dew like the bushes camouflaging them, she seems to be viewing death at a distance, with patience and even—oh, the mystery of those fluttering eyelids, the sharp shadows in the corners of her eyes!—even with irony.

Open doors, washing, barns, man's imprint, biblical dawn in which the centuries jostle, how the whole dazzling mystery of the morning deepens into the mystery cropping out on those wasted lips of hers! Let the mystery of man only emerge from that enigmatic smile, and the resurrection of the earth becomes nothing more than a pulsating backcloth.

I now know the meaning of the ancient myths about the living snatched from the dead. I can scarcely remember what fear is like; what I carry within me is the discovery of a simple, sacred secret.

Thus, perhaps, did God look on the first man . . .